FERAL
CURSE

BOOKS BY
CYNTHIA LEITICH SMITH

THE TANTALIZE SERIES

Tantalize

Eternal

Blessed

Diabolical

THE FERAL SERIES

Feral Nights

Feral Curse

Feral Pride

FERAL
CURSE

CYNTHIA LEITICH SMITH

CANDLEWICK PRESS

Copyright © 2014 by Cynthia Leitich Smith
Epigraph © 1987 by Robert A. Heinlein
© 2003 by The Robert A. & Virginia Heinlein Prize Trust, reprinted
with permission by The Robert A. & Virginia Heinlein Prize Trust

Photographs on pages ii–iii copyright © Image Farm Inc.

First paperback edition 2015

Library of Congress Catalog Card Number 2013946609
ISBN 978-0-7636-5910-3 (hardcover)
ISBN 978-0-7636-7664-3 (paperback)

14 15 16 17 18 19 BVG 10 9 8 7 6 5 4 3 2 1

Printed in Berryville, VA, U.S.A.

This book was typeset in Minion Pro.

Candlewick Press
99 Dover Street
Somerville, Massachusetts 02144

visit us at www.candlewick.com

For Aunt Gail,
who taught me that Story lingers
in antiques and historic homes

HOW YOU BEHAVE TOWARD CATS HERE BELOW
DETERMINES YOUR STATUS IN HEAVEN.

—ROBERT A. HEINLEIN

KAYLA

TONIGHT I FINALLY BARE MYSELF — my whole self — to Benjamin Bloom.

"You wanted to tell me something?" he nudges, impatient.

I do. I insisted on our meeting here this evening at Town Park, supposedly to drink in the glorious violet and peach sunset, before moving this cozy party of two up the hill to my house, to my bedroom, to be precise. It's my parents' twenty-fifth anniversary, so they're celebrating this weekend at the fancy four-star resort off Highway 71.

Meanwhile, we're indulging in a celebration of our own.

Unsupervised at Casa Kayla, I might've lost myself in the heat and slick boy muscles before getting the truth out.

Being sort of in public will guarantee I control my animal urges, at least up to a point. The fine hairs on my skin are already quivering.

Taking a breath, I gently set a gold cat's-eye gemstone in the center of Ben's palm.

"That's it?" His laugh is gentle. "I was worried you were going to break up with me."

"On Valentine's Day?" I exclaim, touched by his rare show of vulnerability.

We've talked about tonight, planned it. I ordered a sheer white mesh-and-lace baby-doll nightie online — and then hovered over my mailbox to snag the package the moment it arrived. He picked up protection at the grocery store off the highway. We sent each other texts that counted down the days . . . and nights. As we touched ourselves, we imagined touching each other.

Ben uses the flashlight app on his phone to examine my gift. "What's this?"

I glance at the historic bridge and the state highway bridge beyond it. "A secret."

"Sweet." Ben sets down his phone and unties the slim leather cord from around his neck. He slides off the shark-tooth pendant and tosses it into the river. Then he threads the mounted cat's-eye and puts the cord back on again. Remembering his manners, he adds, "Thanks."

Ben clearly thinks the gemstone is his Valentine's Day present, my equivalent of the dozen glittery blue roses he had delivered to my house this morning. "Listen," he begins, "I won't be upset . . . disappointed, of course, but not mad . . . if you changed your mind about—"

"No, no," I assure him. "It's nothing like that."

My memories of Ben go all the way back to bilingual Montessori school, though in a town this small, I'm sure we met earlier. At church or Doc Petrie's office or the annual Pine Ridge Founders' Day weekend festival. My constant competition, he beat me by one day for best attendance in second grade, by one vote for freshman class president. But every year, I took first place in the district science fair. As sophomores, we both made all-state in our sports—me in track and cross-country, him in football and baseball. I was keeping score, and so was he. We relished it.

Then the news hit that his dad wouldn't be returning from Afghanistan, that the body was being shipped home in a flag-covered box. It was our town's first military loss in generations.

The day after, Ben disappeared. He did that when he was upset. It was the same when he overshot that pass and we lost to Spirit High, only this time his mother was at her wit's end.

I told myself I wasn't worried, that I'd scold him for being selfish. Well, maybe not scold, given the circum-stances. But I'd drag his hot hiney home so Mrs. Bloom could start trying to breathe again. The least I could do, I'd thought, practically my responsibility.

3

I tracked Ben to the top of the water tower, where he was half drunk on a bottle of Cuervo and smoking a pack of Marlboros, even though he didn't drink, even though he'd never smoked before. Losing his father changed Ben. It made him less trusting of authority figures, of the way the world worked. He was proud of his father's sacrifice, but he still struggled with the meaning of it. It took six more months before I saw his smile again. Finally, it was aimed at me.

Ben and I first kissed last Fourth of July, seated on this same Mexican blanket at this same spot on the matted, dry grass between the water and the park. He said he'd been thinking about doing that for a long time. Kissing, letting his fingertips fall, seeking, between my thighs.

Our first real date was Austin City Limits. He's wearing the black concert T-shirt tonight.

Before long, kids at school started calling us "Kayben" like we were celebrities.

It's been so perfect. Okay, an eyebrow or two may have lifted at him being white and me black, but our parents had been best friends since before we were born, and nobody dared to say "boo" about it in public. I only hope what I'm about to tell him next won't ruin everything.

"Then what is it?" he presses, leaning closer on the blanket. "What's wrong?"

"I . . ." The speech I rehearsed sticks in my throat. "You see . . ."

4

I'm being ridiculous. Ben loves me. I should come right out and say it.

I will. I do. "I'm a Cat."

Ben slides his palm alongside my hip and squeezes. "Meow."

Typical. "An *actual* Cat, you know, with whiskers and a tail."

As he moves in for a kiss, I stop him with two firm fingertips to the chest. "An *Acinonyx jubatus sapiens,* a spotted werecat. Not my parents, just me."

I can deal with being the First Daughter of Pine Ridge, with my father being one the few African-American mayors in Texas, and how much talk there is about all of that, especially since Dad hinted to the *Capital City News* that he might run for the Texas statehouse.

It gets tedious, but fine. I'm used to it. But what on earth would I do if the fact that I'm a werecat went not only public but viral? It's the kind of thing that would make INN. And my *Homo sapiens* mom and dad would be ruined, all because of me.

Just in case, I spell it out for Ben. "My parents are human beings like you."

I'm an only child, and he knows I'm adopted. Everybody knows. When we were babies, our church held a town-wide fund-raiser to help pay for my parents' trip to Ethiopia to bring me home. As much as I trust Ben, I'd never risk their safety. Worst-case scenario, I'll lie and say they didn't know my species. I'll claim that I managed to hide it, even from them.

Ben pinches his brow. It's not horror — he's confused. "You're kidding."

The sun is all the way down, and my night vision is so much better than his. He can't read my expression. I angle myself so I'm facing the water. The river walk, the park, and, up the hill, our small town's historic district are all behind me. That seems appropriate somehow.

From here, I can study the dense forest across the river where I sometimes run wild, all heat and instinct, in animal form. I love that. I live for it.

More than anything, I want to share that side of myself with him.

God, please let him be okay with this. I owe him the truth first, before we . . .

I risk a sideways glance. Bang-up job, Kayla. He still looks baffled.

Fine. I'll show him, then. Lighting up his phone, I angle it at my face and partially free my animal form, releasing my saber teeth, my gold-spotted black fur, and my matching gold Cat eyes. He's in no danger. My control is excellent. But that doesn't mean he won't be afraid.

I hear his sharp intake of breath.

I pray Ben recognizes *me*. Sure, I'm from another branch on the family tree, but I'm still his Kayla, the girl he's known his whole life, the first girl he's ever truly loved.

And I'm as naturally born as he is.

He can't believe what the media says about us, the lies in books and movies. He must know that when our minister condemns shape-shifters, he's preaching politics, not Gospel.

But does he? Ben is a good Christian boy. When we decided to take our relationship to the naked level, we had to pray about it first.

It doesn't mean he won't, but there's no real reason for him to freak out. Shifters aren't magical or demonic. Many of the Lord's creatures can transform. Frogs can change their gender. Snakes can change their skins. So what if we can change on the cellular level? Creation is ever the more glorious for its variety. Ever more miraculous.

Ben reaches to touch the gemstone around his neck, and I feel a flicker of doubt.

I'd feel less vulnerable starkers and spread for his approval.

The hopeful part of me is still looking forward to that.

"Say something," I whisper, fully retracting the shift. "Please."

Ben kisses me instead, brushing his lips against my lips and his insistent tongue against my uncertain one. It's as much reassurance as passion. "I'm so proud of you," he says. "You're incredibly brave to confide in me like this. I won't let you down."

Relief loosens my muscles. I couldn't have asked for a better response.

"I'm glad that you trust me." Ben rises to his knees, reaching for my hands, and I position myself, likewise, facing him. He says, "This doesn't change anything between us."

Having braced myself for his next declaration of love, it comes as a shock when he adds, "We'll find a cure, Kayla, a way to end this nightmare. You don't have to go on like this."

Oh, sweet baby Jesus. Ben not only thinks it's possible to "fix" me, to somehow transform me into a human girl, he's already trying to figure out how to make that happen. "You don't understand," I say. "I *like* who I am. I was *born* a Cat. That's a good thing."

Ben stands, and the air chills between us. "No, that's the devil talking."

With that, he leaves, sprinting across the park, past the picnic tables, barbecue grills, and antique Western carousel, abandoning me in the darkness, kneeling and alone.

The next morning, in a state of near panic, I text Ben: We're finished.

There, it's done. What was I thinking? Why should he be different from anyone else?

What if he tells someone? What if he tells everyone?

My shattered heart be damned. The stakes are enormous. I have to protect my parents, my college plans, my entire future. I could have ruined my whole life.

Then again, what if he feels differently today? What if he panicked and doesn't know how to apologize? What if I'm only making things worse?

I key in another message: Call me. Erase it without sending.

I key it in again, erase it again — a hundred times, a thousand.

I fall asleep with the phone still in my hand, wondering if he hates me now, if we were ever real or something I hallucinated, if the feral part of me he rejected is worthless anyway.

The day after that I'm convinced he never really loved me.

I still love him. I admit it. Who knows? Maybe I always will. Maybe that's the price of true love, the forever ache that comes after it's over. But enough. I'm done. Done, done, done. I have to shut this down before it drives me crazy.

I gather up absolutely everything Ben ever gave me, every single memento of our time together, and toss it all in a cardboard box. I glance down at the toy tricorder, the Houston Astros ball cap, the embossed napkin from Lurie's

Steakhouse, a few dried long-stemmed red roses, the still-fresh bouquet of glittery blue ones, and a photo of us at Homecoming.

I dump the contents in the round concrete fire pit in my backyard, drench it with lighter fluid, and drop in a match. The *whoosh* of flame is bigger than I expected, and my Chihuahua, Peso, freaks out, barking like it's a hell-born fiend, rising to devour us.

I can't avoid Ben. This town's too small for that. And I can't avoid the gossip that'll start once people find out we've broken up. But it's only months until I leave for college.

I can stand it. I can keep breathing. I can keep moving forward.

I'll have to.

"Kayla, love?" It's Mom at the back door.

I expect her to holler at me for nearly setting the yard on fire. I'm almost looking forward to the distraction. Maybe she'll ground me and I'll have a legitimate excuse to hide out at home. Maybe . . .

Something's wrong. Very, very wrong.

Tears haunt her light-brown eyes.

PRHS Quarterback Benjamin Bloom Dead from Lightning Strike

By Geraldine Ackerman

Pine Ridge, Texas—PRHS quarterback Benjamin Jacob Bloom, age 18, was killed by a lightning strike at around midnight on Feb. 15 on the antique "Western" carousel in Town Park.

His body was discovered shortly after 6 A.M. that morning by twin sisters Eleanor and Lula Stubblefield, both age 74, while out for their morning power walk.

Benjamin's mother, Constance Bloom, said she did not realize that her son was missing from their home until the sheriff's office informed her of his death at approximately 7:15 A.M.

"He seemed preoccupied the day before," Mrs. Bloom said. "You know how moody teenagers can be. All I can think is that he snuck out to clear his head and got caught in the thunderstorm."

She added that he'd been known to run off by himself when he was upset.

Coach Floyd Williams said that Benjamin was a talented athlete and honor-roll student who had already accepted a baseball scholarship from Texas Christian University. "All the boys on the team looked up to

11

Ben," the coach said. "He'll never been forgotten at PRHS."

Visitation is scheduled for 7 P.M. Feb. 20 at Mayfield Mortuary. The service will be at 10 A.M. Saturday at Church of the Savior, followed by the burial at Dogwood Trails Cemetery.

In lieu of flowers, the family requests donations to the PRHS booster club.

KAYLA

"IT'S LIKE I KILLED HIM," I whisper to Jess as we take the long, concrete staircase leading downhill from the public-library parking lot toward the winding river walk. We're on our way to the town's official re-dedication of the antique carousel in Ben's memory.

"Kind of risky thing to say to the sheriff's daughter," Jess replies. "Except I'm pretty sure you have no power to call lightning from the sky." She sets a hand on my shoulder. "You didn't kill Ben, and he didn't kill himself. It was God's will."

I can't believe God would do any such thing, even to protect my secret. Still, I'm grateful for the company. Jess Bigheart and I used to be best friends — sleepover, share-your-secrets kind of friends — back when my secrets were so much less dangerous. In elementary school, we were in soccer and ballet together. Her family used to bring me with them to the Austin Powwow every fall, and I still have a photo posted in my locker of the two of us together — me in a denim pencil skirt and a UT T-shirt, her in full regalia to dance Southern Buckskin. She was the one girl in town I could count on to go with me to every super-hero blockbuster and to watch even the odd-numbered Star Trek movies.

Then, when I was thirteen, a hawk made a grab for Peso in my backyard, and my saber teeth came down for the first time — terrifying me, the bird, and my spastic little dog, who spent most of the next week cowering under the porch. I didn't tell anyone but my parents.

Afterward, I gradually pushed everyone else out to arm's length, Jess included. That first year I missed so much school that my mom told the secretary I had mono. At first it was for others' protection — I didn't always have the control over my shift that I do now. Later, it was mostly that I felt so . . . other. At least until Ben, and look how that turned out.

Jess never pressed me for an explanation, though I must've hurt her feelings. She seemed to accept that we were still friends, just not as close. Jess has a big family, though. I see her out with her sisters a lot. I hope that helped. I hope I haven't screwed up everyone I care about.

At the foot of the stairs, Jess and I veer right toward the park and continue on our way. Her companionable silence is a relief. I'm exhausted by everyone else's grief and awkwardness. Unlike most people I know, she doesn't need to fill every blessed minute with nervous chatter.

As we pass the grassy spot where Ben and I last spoke, last kissed, only a stone's throw from the cypress trees planted in memory of 9/11, it's hard for me not to imagine him there, sprawled on the Mexican blanket. If I'd never confided in him, he'd still be alive. He'd still be mine. Maybe even mine forever.

Why did I have to tell him? I could've backed out. Or said I was having my period. Or saving myself for marriage. Or . . . anything, really, absolutely *anything* would've been better than this.

Once Jess and I reach the first of the antique-style streetlights that line the river walk, I say, "We — Ben and I — got in an argument on Valentine's Day."

I didn't tell anyone that we'd broken up, but he might've. Come to think of it, he might've told someone about my Cat heritage, too. I never should've sent that text.

I have to think about damage control. Even by association, the stigma could cost my parents their careers, our home, the respect of everyone they care about.

In . . . I think it's Montana . . . there's a law making it illegal for humans not to report knowledge of a shifter to authorities — a law spawned by rancher paranoia that

Wolves would go after their herds. Like it's not the twenty-first century and werewolves don't shop at butcher counters like everybody else. "I said some things I regret."

Jess winds her thick, curly hair into a messy knot. "Kayla, sweetie, please stop torturing yourself. It's not like you two never got in a fight before. You spent most of your lives bickering, remember? You had no way of knowing what would happen. It's not like anyone else thinks . . ." Her brow creases as if remembering something. "Oh."

"What?" I counter. Jess's older sister manages the new-and-used bookstore on Main, her younger sister waits tables at Davis Family Home Cookin', her brother played football with Ben, her mother owns the beauty parlor, and Jess herself does work for her dad at the sheriff's office. By the transitive property of family dinner conversations, Jess knows everything that goes on in this town. She's not gossipy about it — she just knows.

The fact that she's on the verge of dishing means she thinks I either have a right to the information or it'll be hurtful if I hear it in an unkind way from someone else. "Jess, tell me."

We slow so as not to catch up to the gathering crowd of mourners too quickly, and she says, "When the Stubblefield sisters found . . ."

She doesn't want to say "the body." That's okay. I don't want to hear her say it, either.

Lowering her voice, Jess starts again. "When they

16

found Ben, he'd laid out a pack of matches, a white votive candle, your junior class photo, a dried-up wrist corsage, and an excerpt from a" — she uses her fingers to make air quotes — "'lost companion book to Revelations.' At least that's what it's labeled — it doesn't read like the King James or any other version of the Bible to me. If you want . . ." She hesitates. "I can e-mail you a copy of it."

"You would do that?" I exclaim, too loudly.

At her solemn nod, a few of our classmates turn in unison from the park's picnic area. Spotting me, they clasp one another as if I'm a ghost. I've been getting that reaction a lot since Ben died, as though I'm his widow instead of his girlfriend. Or ex-girlfriend, to be precise.

God, I don't need this right now, but it would've stirred more talk if I hadn't shown.

Five pretty, misty-eyed girls in crisp black dresses rush toward us, all open arms and consoling words. Did I resent them only moments ago? I take it back.

We are each other's touchstones. Together, we've laid to rest beloved grandparents and pets ranging from goldfish to llamas, but, for a member of our own generation, for one of us, this is the first death. Ben is the first death. It still doesn't seem possible.

I can smell their sorrow and exhaustion. Samantha was his first kiss. Lauren was the first girl he got to second base with (I heard it from her, not him, in the church ladies' restroom — two years before he and I ever dated). Shelby was his lab partner in biology, chemistry, and physics — his best friend who was a girl (as opposed to his girlfriend). She was the one who deciphered me for him (and vice versa), who made sure he didn't do anything stupid.

Ben was theirs in a myriad of ways. We all loved him.

"What's that?" I ask, gesturing at Brittney's clipboard.

As we approach the carousel, she explains, "We're here representing Bloom Forever.

"This is a petition demanding that the carousel be removed from the park as an attractive nuisance."

Brittney's smart. She's been accepted at Rice University. But that language came from her mother, one of our town's four lawyers. Brittney adds, "We believe it would be disrespectful to Ben's memory for it to continue being used for amusement purposes."

Amusement purposes? I accept the offered ball-point pen and scribble my name, but, however disloyal to Ben it might sound, I hate the thought of losing the antique carousel. I love the whimsy of it, the fact that it has a history of its own.

People are determined to do something concrete in response to Ben's death. I get that; I do. But why blame an inanimate object? It's utterly irrational.

Especially since I'm the one at fault.

Then again, I've always felt a certain kinship to the antique ride, a personal link, and there's no rational explanation for that, either.

Beyond the picnic tables and barbecue grills, the carousel itself is turned off, no lights, no robotic organ music, no rotation, though the mirrored panels at the base reflect the same sort of lavender-peach Texas sunset as on Valentine's Day. There are no brightly ornamented, prissy fiberglass horses, either. Instead, it's Western themed, trimmed in a mustard yellow and adorned with wooden figures in the shapes of cougars, deer, snakes, black bears, hares, coyotes, buffaloes, elk, wolves, bighorn sheep, hogs, raccoons, armadillos, otters, and robust brown-and-white paint ponies, positioned as if pulling a rustic wagon — two of each animal, like refugees from Noah's ark, each figure big enough for a grown man to ride, including the two cat figures, carved as if they're running. Running in endless circles.

As the mayor's daughter, I know the ride was appraised and insured at over $750,000.

Last summer Pine Ridge bought the carousel off a traveling carnival as part of the city council's eco-devo plan to lure in more weekend tourists from Austin and Houston.

If we'd had any sort of traditional town square or central park, it might've been installed there. But Pine Ridge grew from the river, and our gathering place is here, along the water.

I feel drawn to the carousel, as if I'm sleepwalking. Meanwhile, Brittney takes away the clipboard and

19

pen. Someone presses a thin white candle into my hand. Someone else lights it.

Giant photos of Ben have been positioned artfully on either side of the ride: Ben suited up as quarterback. Ben in his baseball uniform. Ben as Jesus in last year's Easter play. And worst of all, Ben photoshopped to appear in cap and gown. A peek at the future he'll never have. We'll never have together. It seems blasphemous somehow.

As if from a distance, I hear Jess whispering, "Shock. Kayla's in shock."

She's defending the weirdness that is me.

Later, Jess sends me a scanned-in copy of the so-called "lost companion book to Revelations." No message except "XO," which is how she signs off all her e-mails and texts. I'm not sure why she's risking pissing off her dad by passing it on to me (I'm pretty sure it's considered evidence or at least police business), but I'm profoundly grateful for any insights as to what was going through Ben's head. Unanswered questions always frustrate me, but the ones swirling around his death are pure torture.

I hit PRINT, copy and paste a few sentences into a search engine, and the text pulls up on the Web, on sale for $3.99. It's labeled a ritual, a supposed "cure" for shifters. A spell.

The ingredients were at the scene of his death: a flame, an image of my human form (via my class photo), a stand-in of my Cat form (via a cougar figure on the carousel), and something that was mine but connected us — my red rose wrist corsage from Homecoming.

It's not hard to figure out how he got ahold of it. I hung the dried flowers from the elastic wrist band on the inside door of my locker at school. Ben had the combination, and the doors near the high-school gym would've been unlocked for yesterday's varsity baseball practice.

That such a devout boy resorted to sorcery proves how desperate he was to save me.

I realize now that I should've handled the whole thing differently. I should've brought up the subject of shifters long before what was supposed to have been our big night. I should've talked to him as if I wasn't talking about myself, my species.

I knew Ben. I understood how his mind worked. Or at least I thought I did. If anyone could've convinced him to see me as natural, beautiful, *his Kayla,* it would've been me.

Not every religion considers me an abomination. Even within the various branches of Protestantism, it varies church by church, preacher by preacher. I could've drawn support from that. Ben's faith wasn't blind. When interpretations conflicted, he asked hard questions.

We both studied Leviticus, but neither of us believed that God hates shrimp.

Over the holidays, I watched a Web film, a documentary about a family named Cunningham, who're *Nuralagus rex sapiens* living openly in a quaint lakeside town called Windermere in England. I loved how they were depicted as everyday, otherwise normal people and how their surrounding human community totally embraced them, hoppy feet and all.

Maybe if I had shown that to Ben, we could've talked about it and . . .

Then again, I'm not from a species of giant wererabbits.

I'm a werecarnivore, a werepredator.

Big Cats are scarier than big Bunnies.

As I move the cursor to log off, I notice a link to the National Council for Preserving Humanity, and I can't resist clicking to see what the haters are up to now.

Skimming, I can tell that they're getting bolder, more ambitious — targeting city and county commission seats, school boards, and state legislatures. It's a smart, insidious strategy. I've heard Dad talk countless times about the power of grassroots politics.

Over half the country considers the NCPH a bunch of crackpot alarmists, conspiracy theorists. But they've got a growing membership and heavyweight financial backing.

Besides, there's nothing the mainstream media likes more than to paint shifters as bogeymen. One of the NCPH spokespeople appears on some twenty-four-hour news station or another every other night, and they're not alone in their bigotry. Only last week, the History Channel aired a program claiming that Nostradamus foretold of a shifter in the desert who'd bring on the apocalypse.

As I skim the NCPH political blog, Peso scrambles onto my platform bed to snuggle. I pull him onto my lap, comforted by the puppy love. Other dogs are instinctively wary of me, which makes sense, given that they can scent out what I am. But I hand-raised Peso. He associates Cat with safety and love.

The latest NCPH post discusses proposed legislation that would require door-to-door mass testing to confirm *Homo sapiens* status. Among other things, positive results could lead to tattooed IDs, rescinding driver's and gun licenses, the firing of teachers and clergy, and the "cleansing" of the public schools. There's a lot of talk about "protecting our children."

The most vicious comments argue for genocide and justify it as self-defense.

But the hardest part is that even my enemies know more about what I am than I do.

I've caught wind of another Cat on my parents' undeveloped property across the river, but I've never seen her, never once talked to a single other shifter about, well, anything.

White Plains, New York—The mauled body of Jacinda Finch, age 4, was found March 1 in a wooded area of Westchester County, New York, following a five-day search.

Jacinda was the only child of Catchup founder and CEO Reginald Finch and his ex-wife, Chloe Finch-Bjorkman of White Plains and Palo Alto, Calif.

A White Plains City Police spokesperson would say only that Jacinda appeared to have been the victim of a wild animal or shape-shifter attack.

YOSHI

"IF SOME HOT YOUNG TART waltzes in, you'd best keep your pants on," Grams warns. "I know how it is with you and your degenerate animal passions."

Grams is huge on shifter pride, except when it comes to *my* animal passions.

Polishing the glass jewelry case, I make a noncommittal noise.

A couple of months ago, my grandmother moved to Texas from Butler County, Kansas, and bought out the previous owners of Austin Antiques. A giant, freestanding, manila-colored brick rectangle in the middle of a strip-mall parking lot wouldn't have been her first choice, but it was a well-established business at this location and for sale.

She kept the blah name and set up her psychotically over-pruned, overpriced bonsais on a shelf beneath the three gold-framed, beveled mirrors on the wall behind the front counter.

Since then, we've attracted exactly five customers under the age of thirty — one tween-age comic collector, one cute Latina bride seeking a vintage "hair bob," a gay couple who selected an Italian Florentine tray, and a straight couple who bought a 1920s Arts and Crafts desk, stripped of its unfortunate lemon-yellow paint job. Long story short, we're painfully low on hot young tarts.

Don't get me wrong. I fully understand where Grams is coming from. Until a few months ago, when I lived with her on our Kansas farm, I was infamous for my tomcatting ways. A heartbreaking, lovemaking wonder stud with irresistibly touchable black hair.

Not so much lately. Well, the hair is still there. But I've been nursing . . . not a broken heart, exactly . . . more like a cracked one. Yeah, that's it, a hairline fracture of the heart.

"And don't burn the place down, either," Grams scolds, checking the cash drawer one last time. Memo to self: Never share travel stories with your grandmother.

She strolls out from behind a glass counter filled with lace gloves, cameo necklaces, and polished gold pocket watches. "The ladies are hunting for state-souvenir thimbles." Gesturing at the customers toward the back of the store, Grams whispers, "Delilah is apparently collecting."

More penny-ante stuff. Last week they were after blue glass bottles.

Grams adds, "Melly is armed with a new price guide. Jolene has pictures of her pudgy bulldog in a hot-pink tutu, and it's as ugly as sin."

Me and Grams do have a few things in common. For one, we're not dog people.

"How 'bout the new dealer?" I ask. When I strolled in after school, a big guy with a big beer belly and a big belt buckle was staging a booth toward the back.

"Just left," Grams declares with her hands on the front-door push-bar. "You should go familiarize yourself with whatever treasures he's offering."

"Treasures" my sweet Cat booty.

Repressing a sigh, I say, "Fine, I'll check out the booth and flirt with the old ladies."

Anything beats doing pre-calc homework, especially on a Friday night, and, after all, this is a family business. God help me, I'll probably inherit it someday.

"See that you do." With that, Grams cuts out to meet her much-preferred grandchild, my big sister, Ruby, along with Ruby's girlfriend, Erika, at a seafood joint on Lake Austin.

Ruby has invited me to move in with her, but she and Erika are in love, three's a crowd, and Grams and I do a pretty good job of staying out of each other's way. Most of the time.

Working every day after school and on weekends sucks, but there's a HELP WANTED sign in the window. I'm hopeful of eventually getting back some semblance of a life.

I weave through the maze of booths to number 66.

This isn't a bad antiques mall, if you're into that sort of thing — roomy with crappy fluorescent lighting and cracked manila-colored tile floors. We offer purple acai iced green tea in hot weather and likewise-flavored hot tea in cold (not that it ever gets really cold). When Grams is feeling generous, she serves complimentary bowls of miso soup, too. The customers always mention all that in our online reviews.

As for the inventory, dealers are showcasing some pop-culture doodads, like vintage Barbie dolls, Princess Diana memorial plates, and *Knight Rider* lunch boxes. Then there are the scads of Hummel figurines and other assorted dust collectors.

The majority of the big-ticket items are furniture pieces, dining-room tables and armoires mostly, along with desks, vanities, buffets, and wobbly brass pole lamps. Jewelry, of course, costume and semiprecious. The rhinestone tiaras move well. Dealer 48 has some groovy sixties stuff like lava lamps and fringed suede jackets.

From two rows over, I hear a singsong voice, "Delilah, do you see what I see?"

"Sure do!" she replies with a sigh. "It's Texas."

Oh, joy. State-souvenir thimbles.

Deciding to schmooze them later, I focus on the newly set-up booth in front of me.

Yowza. I've seen my share of "antiques" over the years — reproductions, fakes, and the real deal — so trust me when I say the new display at aisle 6, booth 6, is not standard fare.

Let's start with the two stuffed, mounted water-buffalo heads. I'm surprised the booth walls can support their weight. I've seen them, water buffaloes, on Animal Planet or whatever, and I'm still astonished by how freaking huge they are in real life. Or their heads are, at least.

Then I glance at the curvy blond mannequin in a fire-engine-red dress, labeled a "tank dress" that the tag claims was once worn by Marilyn Monroe. It's a sexy, ambitious lie.

I begin checking all the tags.

It's easier to hand-sell something with a story — like "made of genuine snakeskin leather from a rattler shot dead by Sam Houston." Or "carved by three blind Aggies, all named Bubba." Or "sported on LBJ's lapel." (When Grams owned a store in Kansas, the claims were more generic, except when it came to *The Wizard of Oz* paraphernalia, but Texans love anything Texas related. No, really, they're obsessed.)

Anyway, customers — make that *collectors* — groove on a tale to tell, so successful dealers pitch them, and when they're not around, they expect us, as landlords, to do the same.

I run my fingers over a mounted swag of green shag carpeting, supposedly left over from the roll that covers a ceiling in Graceland.

Moving to the back corner, I see there's a six-foot-tall, surprisingly tasteful *shoji* screen, painted in cherry blossoms. I push it back to reveal a carousel . . . cat?

A large, hand-carved wooden cat, wearing a leather Western saddle, with an upright pole stuck through it where the thick neck meets the broad back. It's large enough for a man to ride and depicted in a sprinting position. The eyes are yellow-green, like my sister's.

From the get-go, I'm kind of fascinated by the thing. I am, after all, a *Puma concolor sapiens,* and we shifters tend to feel a strong natural affinity to anything reminiscent of our animal forms. After so many generations in hiding, we like to see ourselves reflected in the world. It's one of the many reasons I drive a classic Mercury Cougar.

The tag claims the carousel figure is cursed — a minus in conservative Houston but a mega plus in funky Austin — and goes on to say a teenage boy died on the carousel in an electrical storm and that the ride was broken up and sold off in pieces.

It's not total BS this time. I heard something about that, the guy's death, a couple of months ago on the local TV news. He was a high-school football star, and people take football damn seriously around here. If I'm remembering right, it went down in some nothing small town an hour or so outside of Austin.

A shame — what happened to him and, for that matter, to the carousel. If the rest of the ride was in as good condition as this cat figure, it would've been something to see.

I rest my palm on the pole, inspecting the other side for chipped paint or other damage.

Looks fine. Underpriced, though. The dealer should be able to get —

White-hot energy seeps into my hand. I gasp, wincing, as it travels up my arm, snakes across my shoulders, and, in a blinding flash, consumes my entire body.

KAYLA

THIS AFTERNOON KICKS OFF Founders' Day weekend in downtown Pine Ridge, and three blocks away from the festivities, strolling home through my historic neighborhood, I can still hear the Brazos Boys jamming to a Willie Nelson tune.

The residential streets are lined with cars, both the locals' and a growing number from all parts of Central Texas. The economy is still puttering. Regional getaways are the hottest thing in travel, according to Dad. The B&Bs are booked solid. So are the chain hotels along the highway.

I like the energy, the activity. It makes me feel a little more anonymous than usual, grateful that people have something to talk about besides the tragedy of Kayben.

I spent the last few hours volunteering at the Adopt-a-Friend booth, offering up kitties, pups, and one hefty rabbit to good homes. Sure, it meant taking a lavender-scented bubble bath and rubbing dots of Peso's canned food on my pulse points to mask my Cat scent. But I didn't mind. Least I could do; that's where I got Peso.

Now I'm starving, the cook-off contest doesn't start until dawn tomorrow, and my mother doesn't believe funnel cakes qualify as a food group. She insisted that I hightail it home for family dinner as usual. Never mind that, outside of election season and the Fourth of July, there's no busier working weekend in Dad's year.

At the corner of Cedar and Main, I pause to sip sweet tea from a straw and watch the moving-company truck pull out of what used to be Ben's gravel driveway. The house has already sold. His mother is relocating to Tualatin, Oregon. Her younger sister owns a preschool there.

It's been about ten weeks since Ben died. Mrs. Bloom says she wants a fresh start.

I think she's running from the memories.

I don't blame her. No matter how hard, it's key to focus forward. Otherwise, we could spin in grief for the rest of our lives. New-student check-in at Cal Tech is exactly four months from today. I've got a studio apartment (with a Murphy bed!) already lined up and a stack of new office supplies ready to pack. I love office supplies, color coding, and, for that matter, packing.

I considered living in a dorm, but a shape-shifter needs more privacy than that. What if I had a bad dream and accidentally started to shift in my sleep?

I'm no longer mad at Ben, not for reacting the way he did to my secret or for that ridiculous "cure" spell or even for dying. Burning his stuff, the remnants of our memories together — that was enough. I don't feel the need to burn down his house or anything, especially since no Bloom will ever live there again. I still feel sort of responsible for his death, but the love part . . .

The love part is murkier. I'm not even sure who I'm mourning, the real Ben or the person I thought he was. But when I promised to love him forever, I meant it. And it wasn't contingent on him loving me back or even being part of my life.

It's something I can do to honor him, to own whatever we were together. I can love him for the rest of my life, quietly, with dignity, no matter how much it hurts or whether anyone else knows it. There's no such thing as an expiration date on forever.

At least Ben did me one favor: he kept my secret to himself. Or, at least, if he did tell someone, he chose well — somebody who either didn't believe him or is keeping it quiet. It's been more than two months. I would have heard otherwise by now.

Beneath the canopy of budding pecan trees, I force

myself to turn away from what used to be Ben's home and continue down the uneven sidewalk toward mine.

Mr. Roberts waves at me from the rocker on his front porch, and I wave back. Come morning, he'll be dressed in his Marine uniform, marching with the other Korean War vets in the parade, or at least strolling proudly.

Pine Ridge is my hometown, and I will miss it. Once I'm off to college, I'll return for visits, of course, holidays, maybe another summer or two. Still, I'm already thinking about top-tier engineering internships across the country. Maybe a semester abroad. Tokyo or Berlin.

Internet rumor has it that no city in the world is as welcoming to shifters as Paris.

Who knows? Maybe I'll minor in architecture or art history.

I'll focus on my studies. I'm graduating at the top of my high-school class. I'm a National Merit semifinalist. I've got a full ride, tuition, and books. I'll make my parents proud.

Another block and I hear the crying boy well before I can see him. I recognize my mother's voice, speaking in low, soothing tones, trying to coax him into our house.

What on earth? Picking up the pace, I quickly round the corner and see the two of them seated on the front step of my family's two-story, newly painted white Victorian. The stranger is a long-limbed teenager with sunlit dark hair, his lanky body bent in grief.

Is he a friend of Ben's? A relative who missed the funeral?

At the sight of me, his chin is up, his nostrils flare, and he freezes in place, his limpid brown eyes wide open.

Peso, barking and waggling with glee at my return, meets me at the front gate of our picket fence and begins frantically hopping on his hind legs, begging for attention.

"Who's your friend?" I call to my mother, bending to scratch my dog behind the ears.

I pause, savoring the wind. The stranger isn't human. He's a shifter.

Or maybe I should call him a "wereperson." I've read online that shifter-rights advocates prefer that word, using "were" as shorthand for shape-changer, though it literally means "man."

I don't want to offend him, especially since he's so miserable. I've always been able to read emotions better than most, but sorrow is practically radiating from the guy.

Sorrow and a hint of fear.

My first in-person encounter with another shifter. Wow.

"He says his name is Darby," Mom replies in a measured voice. "I think he may be lost."

Or mentally challenged, my mother's tone suggests. Clearly emotionally unhinged. But not dangerous, and even if he is, Mom knows my Cat strength outstrips anyone in town.

My mother addresses her next comment to our guest.

"Darby, this is my daughter, Kayla. She'll sit with you while I make a few calls."

Darby hasn't moved, but he's muttering something. He appears to be wholly focused on me, tears leaking down his face like whatever's wrong, it's my fault somehow. "Unworthy." That's what he's saying. "Unworthy, unworthy . . ."

Is he talking about me or himself?

With a quick nod and a tight smile, I promise to look after Darby while Mom tries to figure out where he came from and what to do with him.

We can't turn an unstable teenage shape-shifter over to just anyone. "Wait," I say. "Give me a few minutes, okay?"

Mom fiddles with her gold square earring. "Just a few," she breathes. Then she whistles to Peso, who trots in after her, giving Darby wide berth along the way.

After thinking it over a minute, I take her place on the step and say, "Howdy."

No response, but Darby is slightly shaking. His hairline and underarms are damp. I wonder if I should get him a glass of water. "Where are you from?"

I'm sure Mom already tried to get that out of him, but apparently, he at least shared his name. That gives me hope of learning more. "Why are you here?"

If he's not local, Darby wouldn't know my mother is the go-to person in Pine Ridge. Granted, she's the one who sells real estate and Dad's the one who runs the city, but on the latter front, only technically. This is her hometown. Dad's originally from south Dallas. My parents met on base in South Korea and settled here after they got out of the Air Force.

"Unworthy," Darby goes on. "Help me, my love. Help me, please."

My love? "Help you how?" I ask.

Antlers burst from the top of his head.

Antlers. In broad daylight. In front of my house.

"Stop!" I exclaim, glancing to check whether anyone's around. "What do you think you're doing? You can't. You just *can't*—"

"Kayla," calls a voice from the sidewalk. "What is wrong with that boy?"

It's Sheriff Bigheart, Jess's dad, likewise on his way home for dinner. He's a trim, efficient man who somehow keeps getting elected despite the unsettling fact that he's an Oklahoma football fan.

This is not good. The sheriff may adore me, but he has an infamously reliable BS meter. I'd never dare to lie to him if the situation weren't desperate.

"He's applying for a job at the Christmas shop," I reply, patting Darby's shoulder. Is he still shifting? Yes, God, his nose is starting to morph out. "Or he was going to, but you know how it is—bad economy. Nobody's hiring, and he's taking it hard."

"The Christmas shop?" the sheriff echoes. "Well, you

can't fault the kid's enthusiasm." He scratches his chin. "Hang in there, son! Times are bound to get better."

Grateful I have a big front yard, I forcibly lift Darby to his . . . hooves . . . and half escort, half carry him to the house entrance. He's lanky, awkward to hold, and heavily muscled, but I've got more power in my arms, legs, and shoulders than most car engines. Or at least it feels that way. "You're absolutely right," I yell over my shoulder. "I'll get some of Mom's cheesecake pie in him, and he'll be feeling jim-dandy in no time."

Jim-dandy. Just brilliant, Kayla. It's an expression Grandma Morgan uses. I'm not even sure what it means. At least "pie" is convincing. It's the quintessential remedy hereabouts for just about anything.

"Who *is* that?" Sheriff Bigheart asks, leaning against the fence. "I don't recognize him."

At the same time, I shove Darby into my foyer. Blocking the street view, I wave good-bye — with a big smile — and, pretending I didn't hear that last question, slam the front door.

Then I count to three and turn to face the naked, fur-covered boy, rocking in a fetal position on the hard-woods. Darby must've managed to wiggle out of his clothes before they got thrashed. They're in a pile beside him. He's still saying it: "Unworthy of your love."

YOSHI

HOLY CRAP ON A CRACKER! I'm flat on my ass, my ears are ringing, and every muscle burns. Wiping a dab of blood from my nose, I realize I've landed (appeared?) on a carousel platform. The upright poles and seat figures have all been removed. A large, heavy plastic tarp has been draped over the whole thing and secured to the ground with metal stakes.

I'm guessing that the fact this — whatever the hell it is — happened to me right after I touched the carousel-cat figure at the antiques mall is not a coincidence. It's magic.

I hate magic.

I let out a long, shaky breath. I'm sore all over, but I can see as well as I ever could in the dark, and I still know who the president is. My ears prick at the sound of rockabilly music.

With a groan, I force myself to my feet, raise a hunk of the tarp, and duck out under it. I take in the surroundings, the empty park grounds ahead and the tall woodsy hill behind me. Checking my digital watch, I see that no real time has passed since I left Grams's antiques mall. Whatever happened, it was instantaneous. Or my watch is malfunctioning.

Where am I? With pained steps, I take another look at the carousel. I pull the tarp partially back up again and am struck by the sheer strangeness that the ride has been turned into a sort of giant picture frame featuring huge images — taller than me — all of the same guy.

He's young . . . I'm guessing about my age . . . dressed for football, for baseball, in a crown of thorns and a saintly white robe, and, finally, in a graduation cap and gown.

I draw my phone from my back jeans pocket and confirm the time reading on my watch. Then, using GPS, I locate myself, spitting distance from Main Street in Pine Ridge, Texas, which apparently is about an hour southeast of Austin.

Damn. Glancing around, I spot the lights at the top of the ridge and a long concrete staircase leading up. The ringing in my ears has faded. Now I can hear not only the music but also voices talking from above as well as flowing water and the honking of a goose down here.

Geese? And wood ducks. Yeah, there's a river over there, reduced to a stream by the drought. And a highway beyond that.

Lacking any better ideas, I call my best friend, Aimee, also known as She Who Cracked My Heart — not that best-friendship is a bad consolation prize. I know she's working tonight, but it's either her or Ruby, who's out with my grandmother. I'll be in enough trouble when Grams finds out I left Austin Antiques unlocked and unattended. No need to rush that.

When Aimee answers, I say, "You know our pact to give a shout out if we ever find ourselves kidnapped, beaten up, or somehow targeted by the mysterious supernatural?"

"As opposed to the regular, run-of-the-mill supernatural?" Over the clangs and shouts of the restaurant kitchen, I hear her say, "Clyde, cover for me. It's Yoshi."

I'm sure he's thrilled to hear it. Clyde is her boyfriend. They have part-time jobs as dishwashers at Sanguini's on South Congress. He and I aren't best pals, but we play nice for her sake. Usually.

"Start talking," she tells me. "Start with you. Do you still have a pulse?"

I can imagine her bustling out of the commercial kitchen, fielding the call in the rear parking lot. "I think I'm all right," I reply. "Nothing's bleeding or broken." My nose is still spotting, but it's not bad.

I catch sight of a middle-aged lady. She's jogging this way on the river walk, wearing earbuds, and, under her breath, singing along to an early Carrie Underwood song.

Hiding behind one of the enormous mounted photographs, I whisper what I know so far.

Aimee exclaims, "You beamed an hour away?"

" 'Beamed'?" I reply.

"Teleported," she clarifies. "Like with a transporter from *Star Trek*. Only since this isn't the twenty-third century, we're definitely talking magic."

I laugh. "Yeah, I already figured that much out."

After a pause to digest the situation, she adds, "I can cut out of here if I have to. Do you want me to come and pick you up?"

"Isn't your dad in town this weekend?" Aimee's been going on about his visit for weeks.

"No." Her voice sounds tight. "He canceled again. Something about media training at work. On the upside, he's finally sending child support and he's caught up on all of his back payments." She sighs. "Really, Yoshi, it's no big deal. I can tell my manager I'm leaving now."

Aimee's only a sophomore. She doesn't have a car, but she could borrow one or pick up mine at Grams's

43

antiques-mall parking lot. Months ago I gave Aimee my extra set of keys in case of an emergency. This more than qualifies, except . . . "Have you ever driven on a highway?"

"Technically, no, but I have tons of experience asking for rides."

Right then, a tiny dog, panting hard, races across the picnic area. It's being chased by . . . it's too big to be a wolf. That's a wereperson. A werewolf? No, it's smaller, more slender, the ears are pointier, the tail bushier, and it has a bounce to its step. His coat's reddish brown with white fur around the lips and a tawny belly, but he's bigger than a werefox.

Coyote. Yeah, the wind-borne scent confirms it's a werecoyote in full animal form.

What's he thinking? I detect the faintest scent of Deer, of Cat, of the Coyote himself, but this is human-controlled territory. It may be dark, but the whole landscape is heavy with the scent of *Homo sapiens*. Besides: small dog, big bully. I may not be a dog person, but I hate bullies. "Aimee, I'll have to call you back."

I shove the phone in my pocket and take off. A short-legged little pooch like that has zero chance of outrunning a Coyote, but it's managed to put a play-scape — specifically a spiral orange plastic slide — between itself and the large predator. When the shifter zigs, the dog zags.

"Hey, asshole," I begin, closing the distance. "Step away from the Chihuahua."

44

The Coyote snarls at me. I can tell by his eyes and tone that he understands what I'm saying, word for word, just fine.

Unless something's gone terribly wrong, werepeople don't lose our sense of self when we shift, and unlike our distant animal kin, he can't tree this kitty by intimidation.

I can flash to Cat form in a heartbeat and with no recovery time. It's all natural, a family predisposition that qualifies as a superpower. Or at least it's fun to think so. But I won't turn full *Puma concolor sapiens,* not this close to civilization. Not unless I have no choice in the matter.

It's not just about passing as human. A cop or random citizen might panic at the sight of what they assume is a cougar and shoot. So I bare just my saber teeth and claws.

The Coyote responds with a lame bark-screaming sound, tucks his furry tail, and retreats sideways. I take a step, two, in his direction, and he bounds off toward the river.

Loser. Senses on high alert, I watch until I'm sure he doesn't circle back around.

Then I crouch, trying to make myself less intimidating, and address the terrified pup. It's practically burrowed into the ground under the lowest part of the slide.

After a moment's hesitation, I extend the back of my hand toward its nose. I wish I had food to offer. Hell, I probably smell scarier to him than the Coyote did. But he whines and wiggles forward, which is so brave of him.

Humans may not be great at picking shifters out of a

crowd—thank God. But animals can. I can't help wondering why the wee pup isn't more afraid of a werecat.

"Hey there, little fella," I begin. "My name's Yoshi, and I promise not to hurt you. But I think we're both lost." The name tag hanging from his rhinestone leather collar reads PESO.

KAYLA

AS FRIDAYS GO, this one sucks. Not only is a teenage were-deer wailing at my kitchen table, my dog, Peso, is nowhere to be found.

As I'm peering out the back-door window, Darby says something semi-coherent. "You might as well go. I can't hold on to you. You're lost to me forever. Unworthy. I'm unworthy. Unworthy, unworthy, unworthy of your love."

Mom glances over from the sink counter, where she's chopping carrots.

Dad was supposed to be at the historic Opera House to announce the winner of the Little Miss Pine Ridge Pageant seven minutes ago. Instead, he presents Darby with a cup of hot cinnamon tea. "You sure you've never seen him before, pumpkin?"

"Yes," I say. "Positive." I wish he'd stop asking me that.

Peso is tiny. He could get hit by a car or . . . Then again, I can't bail now. The Deer is completely unstable. He could impale one of my parents on his antlers . . . I think.

I'm starting to lose my patience. I tend to get that way when a situation turns illogical and exhausting. "Who *are* you, Darby?" I don't even know if that's his first name or last.

He wipes his eyes. "I'm in the school band. I play the clarinet."

How very not helpful. Or interesting.

Mom sets a heaping garden salad in front of him. It's a safe bet that a Deer's a vegetarian.

Dad moves to my side. "You find Peso. We'll see what we can do here. Darby may calm down enough to reason with if you're out of the house."

I'm sure the Deer's ears picked up every word. I gut-check my instincts, and feel no sense of danger or urgency except my own concern for my dog. Impaling seems unlikely.

"Call it a plan," I reply, making a run for it out the back. I wince as Darby cries out at my departure. The door shuts behind me with a *bam,* and it's like I can breathe again.

Passing the storm shelter and then beneath my tree house, I rest my gaze briefly on the fresh hole where Peso dug his way out under the fence. His Chihuahua scent is pronounced here, mixed with that of a mystery canine.

The new dog in the neighborhood — I've caught wind of it more than once in the last couple of weeks, outside my school and the public library. Almost like it's following me around, which is silly. It's probably curious, trying to noodle out what I am.

A lot of animals got lost during last autumn's wildfires.

"Peso! Peso!" I jog through my neighborhood, wondering if he's camped out, living large at the taco booth downtown. Everybody loves Peso. Anyone who saw him out and about would keep an eye on him. But this weekend, there are a lot of strangers in town for the Founders' Day festivities.

I'm almost to the library when I hear his familiar barking. "Peso!"

Ahead in the shadows, an athletic male figure appears at the top of the ridge overlooking the park and river walk. He bends to gently set down the wiggly Chihuahua, and I rush to meet Peso halfway, cradling him in my arms, laughing as he licks my nose.

"I take it that's your dog." The voice sounds downright flirtatious.

Great. A pervert. I set Peso down to calm himself. "That's right."

I don't scare easily. Besides, I'm faster and stronger than any human, and anyone who dared to mess with a local girl in Pine Ridge would have to fight off the whole town. All I have to do is scream. This is not the kind of place where people don't want to get involved.

It occurs to me that I'm being melodramatic and probably the guy simply wants a cash reward and that I should really get back home to see how it's going with Darby.

My lips part as the stranger drinks me in with his eyes. For a flush moment, I feel rare and exquisite, but then I realize what he sees in me. Or rather scents.

I casually move in for a closer look. Never before has a Chihuahua-friendly dude this intriguing set foot in Pine Ridge. He smells like the sun on spring grass, and, most important, he's the first male Cat I've ever met. He's Asian or Latino. Dark-wash jeans and a snap-up Western shirt that should look old-school redneck but instead outlines his slender muscles just right. He's sexy. He's breathtakingly sexy. But *another* shifter in town?

"Hi. I'm Kayla. I live here."

Please don't be a pervert.

He raises an eyebrow. "At the library?"

"In Pine Ridge. You're not local, right?" Smooth, Kayla, very smooth.

God, there's so much I want to ask him. I know practically nothing about what it means to be what I — what we — are. I need — make that, I could really *use* — a friend. Someone to trust.

"I'm Yoshi." He lowers his voice so no passing human could hear. "Yoshi Kitahara. You don't happen to know a werecoyote with lousy people skills?"

I briefly register that the name is Japanese and that he looks mixed race. Eurasian, I'm guessing. "Werecoyote?" I shake my head. "Because?"

He glances back toward the river. "Because he tried to eat your dog."

"Peso!" I bend to look my pup over again, running my fingertips across his short, bristly coat. He's panting, skipping in circles. He doesn't seem injured.

I swoop him up again and straighten.

Yoshi asks, "Any ideas as to what's going on?"

"I . . . Lately, I've picked up a new canine scent around town. I dismissed it as a stray."

He rakes a hand through his thick, dark hair. "You think it's the same werecoyote?"

My nod is almost military. It's not like there's a local pack. I realize aloud, "He's been stalking me."

Yoshi insisted on walking me home, and along the way, we decided the Coyote wasn't a problem we could ignore. "Not many werecats are dog people," he observes at my gate. "I'm not."

Humph. If ditching Peso is necessary to functioning in the Cat world, I can live without it.

I've done fine on my own this far.

Yoshi adds, "If you want to track the Coyote, this detour is only giving him more time —"

"I'm *not* bringing Peso with us," I say. "He's been through enough tonight." Gesturing behind the live oak in my backyard, I add, "Stay here. I'll only be a minute."

Yoshi flashes a tantalizing smile. "Too soon to introduce me to your parents?"

I feel myself blush. Is he always like this? I'd bet yes. Good-looking, a shade too cocky, and it's working on me. Can he tell I'm attracted to him? Worse, can he *smell* it? "Stay."

"All right," Yoshi calls as I cross the yard. "But if you tell me to heel, I'm gone."

Very funny. It's a relief to put some distance between us. In light of the Ben fiasco, I've sworn off guys . . . until I meet someone who for sure won't mind that I'm a Cat.

Then again, on that score, Yoshi automatically qualifies. I glance over my shoulder, and he waves at me. Smiles again, even cockier.

I shouldn't have looked.

KAYLA

I LET PESO INTO THE KITCHEN, and he scampers on the Mexican tile floor to his food dish. As I pour in some kibble, Mom comes in. "Ah, good!" she exclaims. "You found him."

I'm close with my parents. I didn't hesitate to confide in them when I first sprouted whiskers and a tail. But given today's drama with Darby, I feel somehow embarrassed about there being another shifter-related problem (in the form of the Coyote) and a new shifter companion (in the form of the Cat) so soon. For the moment, I'll keep both to myself.

"Where'd Darby go?" I ask.

"The Best Western. As luck would have it, they had one cancellation. Darby's brother is driving down in the morning to bring him home to Fort Worth."

"Fort Worth?" I reply. That's — what? — three and a half hours away. "Doesn't Darby have a car in town? How'd he get here?"

Mom grabs a rag and wipes down the table. "He claims all he remembers is having been dragged to some art exhibit with his family at the old stockyards and then coming to his senses at the carousel in our park."

I'm sure somebody's already missing him, probably worried sick. "Okay if I go for a run?" I ask. I'm on the track team, and I ran cross-country in the fall. But in my house, "go for a run" is code for gallivanting around in Cat form on our acreage across the river.

If I wait too long between shifts, it's like an itch beneath my skin.

"Be careful," Mom says, kissing my forehead. "And don't stay out too late."

There's no local predator that can take me on. But theoretically, hunters are a threat, even though we have PRIVATE PROPERTY: NO HUNTING signs posted every fifty yards along the barbed wire.

It's not only that I look like a wild animal. With my spotted coat, I can't pass for a cougar. So, if I'm seen, even if I manage to escape, it's more likely that I'll be recognized as a shifter — in which case, bring on the pitchforks and bloodthirsty mob.

Or it's just as likely I'd be mistaken for an exotic cat who's escaped from an illegal private zoo or owner, which could mean unwanted attention of another sort. I tried to dye my fur once, but it reboots to its natural spotted pattern with every shift.

"I'll be back before you know it." I pause with my hand on the doorknob. "Let's keep Peso inside the house unless someone's with him, at least until traffic lightens up in town."

Mom agrees, and a moment later, I rejoin Yoshi behind the gnarled oak.

He's talking on the phone. "No, no, for the time being, I'm fine in Pine Ridge," he says. "The Chihuahua is fine, too. I ran into his owner, who was out looking for him, and now we're going after the Coyote —" He blinks at me and tells whoever, "I'll call you back."

I hear a faint female voice protesting as he ends the call. "Your girlfriend?" I ask.

It slipped out. Did it sound jealous? Am I jealous?

No, *no*. Ben hasn't been gone that long. It's only normal that I'd be fascinated by another Cat. I almost feel like I can be myself, my whole self, with someone for the first time in my life. Almost. There are too many unanswered questions for me to sink too far into this potential friendship. For the foreseeable future, I'm tabling the whole dynamic.

"*Friend*-friend." Yoshi uses one hand for balance to spring over the picket fence.

"Don't show off," I say, using the swinging gate. "Someone might see —"

"I know how to be careful," he replies.

"Be *more* careful." I gesture down the street. "Sheriff Bigheart lives in that blue house."

That gets his attention, and Yoshi's manner becomes more subdued.

As we skirt downtown, he mentions that he's from Austin. "But only for a few months now. I'm living with my grandmother in a two-bedroom apartment near UT. We don't have a big fancy house."

He says it with a hint of a grudge. Jealous? Competitive? Ben used to compare our houses, too. "Real estate is a lot cheaper here in the boondocks than in Austin."

"I know," Yoshi replies. "In Kansas, we had a big farmhouse and livestock. The animals have been relocated to my sister's land now. She has this giant hog named Wilbur that —" He nods toward the yoga studio. "Friend of yours?"

Jess waves at me, coming out of an evening class. Her mom is waiting for her on the front step. They exchange a few words, glancing our way, clearly curious about my new friend.

"Are you visiting someone in Pine Ridge?" I ask Yoshi, waving back.

"You, apparently," he replies.

I'm in no mood for cryptic. It occurs to me that Yoshi, who I just met, is my only eyewitness source on the supposed werecoyote and that I'm chasing after them both into a badly lit, probably otherwise abandoned park, heavily obscured from downtown by tree and shrub growth. However much I've longed to have another Cat to talk to, I can't automatically assume Yoshi's a safe person. I'm glad that we were seen together and that he knows it.

"That was Jess," I say. "She's one of my oldest friends and the sheriff's daughter."

He nods, his gaze flicking back in that direction. "You have a lot of friends?"

I shake my head. "Not close friends."

"Good," Yoshi says. "Best we keep this between us."

Whatever. We cut across the bank parking lot, and for no apparent reason, I find myself wondering about Cat mating rituals. Are there rituals? Is that what they — we — call it? Mating?

It sounds so animalistic.

At the winding concrete path, I hesitate. "I'm not interested in anything physical."

"I can't promise the Coyote will mind his manners," Yoshi replies. "He scared off easy last time, but that doesn't —"

"No, I mean . . ." I didn't used to suck at this. Before Ben, I was fairly composed—if not especially experienced—around boys. "I'm not interested in getting physical with *you*, romantically or sexually." Wincing, I realize I didn't need to reference sex at all.

Without turning to face me, Yoshi shrugs. "I don't need to come up with elaborate schemes to get girls alone." His tone is matter-of-fact. "You said you thought the Coyote was stalking you. He's bad news, and I'm not the type to let you deal with him on your own."

I'm not sure whether to be embarrassed or annoyed. "Because I'm a girl?"

"Hardly. My sister, Ruby, who's training to be a cop, could kick my ass on any random Tuesday. But have *you* ever been in a real fight?"

Somehow I don't think he'll be impressed that I scared off a hawk. Once. Years ago. "There are shape-shifters in law enforcement?"

Yoshi frowns. "There are shape-shifters pretty much everywhere. Not all of us keep to our own kind. It's a dangerous way to live, but . . ." He begins jogging down the path, and after a moment, I follow. "Over here," he calls, alongside the park play-scape. "You catch his scent?"

I circle in, concentrating. "Yeah." My voice goes hollow. "He's been in my backyard."

"Uh-huh." Leaning against the swing set, Yoshi folds his arms over his chest. "Okay, enough mystery. Let's see what we can rule out. Are you a sorcerer, wizard, alchemist, magician, or non-peace-loving-non-wiccan variety of witch?"

I have no idea what he's talking about. "Absolutely not. I am a Methodist."

Yoshi runs a hand through his shiny hair. "I want to ask you something else. Follow me."

Seconds later, we're standing in front of the antique carousel, or what's left of it. Stripped of the carved animal-shaped figures, it looks like a lonely wood-and-metal corpse.

Yoshi steps up on the platform like that's no big deal, like it isn't some sort of sacred space. He's the first person I've seen do that since Ben died, though of course the Stubblefield sisters and Sheriff Bigheart and whoever installed the photo display must've tromped all over it.

Yoshi extends his arms to both sides. "What do you know about this thing?" He gestures at the photo of Ben in his Jesus costume. "And exactly who is Mr. Wonderful?"

I don't want to have this conversation. "Why?"

Yoshi sinks to sit on the edge of the carousel platform. "This is where I teleported in, after touching a carved cat figure that I'm betting used to be attached to it."

Any other day, I would've dismissed the idea outright.

Tonight, in the moonlight, anything seems possible. Is that how Darby got here? He mentioned the carousel, too. I ask, "Teleported, like on *Star Trek*?"

Yoshi laughs out loud at that, and the genuineness of it prompts me to tell him about Ben and how he died, though I leave out the part about him being my boyfriend. I'm not sure why. It's not that I don't trust myself to talk about it without welling up. I'm past that. I am.

"Yeah," Yoshi says finally. "I remember seeing the story in the news." He opens his mouth like he wants to say something more but can't find the right words.

I nod, letting him off the hook, and then Yoshi and I trace the werecoyote's scent and faint paw prints to the river.

"We should sweep the area," the Cat says. "I'll go this way. You head down there. But don't wander far." He moves toward the bridges, and I do another quick pass through the picnic area before turning in the other direction.

"Over here!" Yoshi calls from the patch of woods between the park and downtown.

I leave the riverbank to meet him on the stairs leading to the parking lot outside the library. "Our Coyote left his clothes on a branch, along with this." Yoshi hands me an ID. "Kitten, say hello to Peter Villarreal of San Antonio, Texas."

Did he really call me "kitten"? I make my way up the stairs to the nearest streetlight for a clearer look, confirming the scent. Peter looks a bit like I'd imagine from his animal form. He's wiry with a prominent nose, pronounced ears, inquisitive expression. He has a dimpled chin and the kind of auburn hair that glints red. I try to imagine him without the beard, given that simply shaving would dramatically alter his appearance.

"Never seen him before," I say. It's like Darby all over again, except more threatening; both shifters seem unduly interested in me. And Yoshi hasn't strayed far since we met.

The Cat is still looking through Peter's wallet, and I see that Yoshi has Peter's phone, too. Pulling out a small piece of rectangular white paper, he says, "This restaurant receipt is for pulled-pork sliders and a Diet Coke. It's dated thirteen days ago, from a *biergarten* in Fredericksburg, Texas."

I've been to Fredericksburg. It's German, quaint, touristy — lots of antiques shops. A popular day-trip and weekend destination in much the same way my dad hopes Pine Ridge eventually will be.

Yoshi hands me Peter's phone, and after fiddling with it for a few seconds, I'm looking at an on-screen image of myself: me on my front porch. I keep forwarding: me playing fetch with Peso, me coming out of my fence gate, walking to school, walking from school, on the church steps, in my mother's new "previously owned" Toyota. It's nothing I hadn't already put together, but the images make it more real somehow. Creepier.

Thinking out loud, I say, "There was a coyote figure on the carousel." Not to mention a deer and a cougar-ish cat. Parallel forms to Peter, Darby, and Yoshi.

Magic at the carousel. Could Ben's spell somehow have brought them here?

"I've got to get home. We should return Peter's stuff to the spot where you found it or he'll know we're onto him."

"He'll know anyway," Yoshi counters. "He'll be able to smell us."

"But he'll be naked," I reply.

A smile tugs at the Cat's lips. "I don't see where that's our problem. I say we keep all this, and he'll come after us, trying to get it back. We can use it to set a trap."

That's inviting trouble, but the Coyote almost killed my dog. His behavior is escalating. He may come after me, or even my parents, next.

YOSHI

ON THE WAY TO HER HOUSE, Kayla tells me about Darby, the mournfully love-struck, skittish Deer she met earlier this evening — a perfect stranger to her before today — and how his animal form was represented by a figure on the carousel, too.

"A real heartbreaker, you are," I tell her. "You think the spell that brought us here may be influencing our behavior and pointing us your way?"

"I was raised to believe in math and miracles, not magic," she says, carrying Peter's wallet, belt, folded clothes, and shoes. "But I can't deny that something strange is happening." Kayla hesitates at the gate. "How about you? Do you feel any different than normal?"

I unleash my trademark smile. "I do find myself strangely fixated on you."

Kayla bites her lip, clearly exasperated, as the silence becomes awkward. Moving into the backyard, I understand that her inviting me to bunk overnight inside the — Jesus — fully restored Victorian mansion would prompt too many parental questions.

It also makes more sense that I stay outside to intercept Peter whenever he makes his move. I cased out her tree house when we swung by earlier with the Chihuahua.

I've crashed in much rougher places. It'll do for tonight.

"I'll be able to smell the Coyote coming." I leap onto a thick branch, showing off how well my Cat agility hangs on in human form. "Trust me, Kayla. He'll never make it to your door." The windows are more vulnerable, but I don't mention that. Coyotes may not climb well in animal form, but in boy shape he's closer to a primate.

Once she hands up Peter's belongings, our bait, I add, "You should get inside. Double-check all the locks." I continue up, adding, over my shoulder, "Go on. Get out of here."

Kayla frowns. But within two minutes of going into her house, she sprints back outside with a sleeping bag, pillow, and leftover barbecue brisket in a doggie bag labeled DAVIS FAMILY HOME COOKIN'. The girl is a saint.

"You don't have to do this," she whispers from the

tree-house entrance. "You could just go home to Austin and forget —"

"Forget having been magically transported over thirty miles?" I reply. "Besides, antiques — cursed or otherwise — are my family business. I may be able to figure this out."

In her moment of hesitation, I can't help studying her. Kayla is a dazzling specimen of womanly Cat flesh. She's got a lean sexiness, high breasts, and the kind of tapered neck that's begging to be nuzzled. She could shake me out of my funk over Aimee.

I wonder what Kayla looks like in Cat form. Just thinking about it, I'm salivating.

"If you say so," she finally replies before hurrying inside for the night.

I jump down, haul up my provisions, devour dinner, and do what I can to settle in.

Inside the tree house, it's fairly civilized, and I revel at being surrounded by her scent. This place offers me a glimpse into the lovely Kayla. Battery-operated lamps and radio, throw rugs, two smiley-face beanbags, a copy of *Mechanical Engineering* magazine, and tacked-up posters of the Cal Tech campus and Scotty from *Star Trek*. Serious geek cred. Aimee would approve.

Must stop thinking about Aimee.

I'm not sure the "friends" thing is working for me.

Then again, do I have any other friends? No.

Anyway, the tree house looks to be a prefabricated

cabin inserted into and among the thickest branches. It's too bad. A simple platform would've offered better visibility and been quicker to launch from if necessary.

Leaving Peter's belongings and Kayla's sleeping bag behind, I scale to the shingled gray roof of Kayla's home. This way, I've got a 360-degree view. It's less comfortable, but that's okay. I'm exhausted, and with an erratic werecoyote on the prowl, I can't afford to doze off.

So it's not a mansion. It's still huge — I'm guessing five bedrooms, all upstairs, and maybe one behind the kitchen on the first floor. It's the kind of place you'd see on a holiday tour of homes.

I glance at my watch and then retrieve my phone to text Ruby, asking that she lock up and tell Grams that I'm staying overnight with a friend. Then I check messages and realize Aimee has called me a half dozen times.

I should've updated her sooner.

"Yoshi!" she exclaims. "You do *not* call someone to say you were magically *teleported* and then call to say you're off hunting an unstable werecoyote and then totally blow her off! I was worried you were dead!" She pauses. "Are you dead?"

"I'm not dead." In fact, I feel more grounded, more myself, just hearing her voice. "Not undead. Not in immediate danger. I met a nice, pretty girl. We took a stroll under the stars, and now I'm at her place. She's a werecat, to boot."

The first female of my species that I've ever met, not

counting Grams, my sister, and my largely theoretical mother. I have crossed paths with a Lioness and a wide variety of other shifters — Grams's barn in Kansas used to be a stop on an underground railroad for werepeople on the run — but my species tends toward the independent and elusive.

Aimee's voice becomes muffled. She's covering the phone with her hand, no doubt updating Clyde on my situation. "Honestly, Yoshi! You didn't call me back because you hooked up with some random —"

"It's not like that," I protest. "She's special."

"Oh, that's good." Aimee's a sucker for romance, and I can't help noting the lack of jealousy in her voice. "But there's something you're not telling me."

"I've gone all white knight, but I can't trust it. I can't trust anything I'm feeling." I've been ensorcelled once before, and it nearly got me killed. Even if it's not Kayla's fault — make that *especially* if it's not Kayla's fault — I've got every reason to be shaken.

"It wouldn't be like you to bail on a distressed damsel," Aimee observes.

Sweet of her to say so. "True," I admit, "but it's more textured than that. I'm also trying to win Kayla's respect. When I came across her copy of *Mechanical Engineering* magazine, my first thought was that I wanted to get into MIT and show her who's —"

"MIT?" Aimee laughs. "Aren't you flunking —?"

"I'm getting all Cs and Ds, but yeah, I might not graduate this spring, and I don't really care. Or at least I didn't. I'm never going to college. We don't have that kind of money and—"

"And you're not that ambitious," she concludes. "How did you handle it?"

"I flirted," I admit. "Flirting is my default mode."

Aimee leaves that comment alone. After I fill her in on the supernatural aspect of the situation, she offers again to leave work and ride in with reinforcements. But more people on the scene could scare off Peter, and I've already set and baited this trap with his stuff.

What might help is more information, and I've got a feeling Kayla's holding out on me. "See what you can find out about Western-themed carousels and any teleportation spells with personality adjustment or brainwashing side effects. I'll call you in the morning."

With that, I settle in to wait for the werecoyote.

A rooster crows at dawn. Kayla and I exchanged cell numbers before she went in. I check my phone for texts. Nothing.

My ears catch a soft crunch of grass. I roll over and glimpse the vague outline of a hand climbing up the oak from behind.

Hello, Coyote.

I've already crept to the edge of the roof by the time the intruder's entered the tree house.

Then I spring to a hearty branch. Extending my claws, I race up until I'm just below the doorway, then fly inside. Peter lets out an *oomph!* as we career together against the wall.

That's when my nose announces that I've made a huge mistake.

Before I can retreat, a pointed cowboy boot slams into my solar plexus.

Lucky shot. I suck in a breath and hit the floor hard, knocked to fully human form. It's darker in here, but my eyes adjust immediately.

As I start coughing, Aimee whispers, "Yoshi! I'm so sorry!" She's holding a Taser gun.

"Shh!" I scold, frantically texting Kayla: False alarm. "Do *not* tase me," I say to Aimee. "I hate when people tase me. What are you doing here?"

"You obviously need my help."

"But—"

"But nothing. It's not like I charge into these situations willy-nilly. I tried to recruit a guardian angel to handle it instead, and go figure: it turns out they answer to a higher power than me."

"Very funny." Still, it was good of her to come. When Aimee said she wanted to be friends, she wasn't brushing me off. She meant it.

At the sound of a screen door opening, I stifle my next cough and struggle to my feet. Aimee and I trade a quick glance and, crouching down, peek out of the tree-house window.

Sure enough, there's a fifty-something balding black man in robe and slippers, holding a shotgun. I'm fast, but not faster than a speeding bullet, and now I have Aimee to worry about, too. By Texas standards, is it a worse offense to be caught in a man's daughter's tree house with said daughter or to be caught in a man's daughter's tree house with someone else's daughter?

Trespass is taken seriously, either way.

Across from us a second-floor window opens. "Dad!" Kayla calls. "It's stray cats. They've been yowling all night. You want me to chase them out?"

"Nah," her dad says, retreating inside. "Go back to sleep and I'll —"

The door closes. Kayla disappears from the window, the lacy white drape fluttering closed.

I whisper, "Is that pork I smell?"

"You must be distracted. I would've thought you'd have picked up on that first." Aimee puts away her weapon. "Javelina chops." She gestures to a brown bag set to one side of the door beside a backpack that I'm hoping holds a couple of changes of my clothes.

"Sure you're not hurt?" I give her a quick half hug. "I thought you were the werecoyote."

"Obviously." She grins up at me. "The wily Coyote?"

"That's not funny."

"Don't be ridiculous. It's hysterical."

I raise her hand to check out the new bling on her finger. It's a ring. Not a fashion ring like my sister sometimes wears. A square-cut pink gemstone surrounded by tiny diamonds. Nothing that Aimee would pick out for herself. "Did Clyde get that for you?"

Rings are serious stuff.

Aimee shakes her head. "My dad, if you can believe it. I guess his new job pays well. He also sent my mom a spa gift certificate for her birthday, and they barely speak. I have no idea what he's thinking."

Maybe he's come to his senses and wants his family back. Aimee's father is a sensitive subject. Moving to unpack my breakfast, I redirect the conversation. "How'd you get here?"

"I took your car."

At least she's okay. "Is my car okay?"

She laughs. "I'm okay. The car's okay. Are you?"

"I'll live." Aimee's been taking martial-arts classes, but lucky shot or no, I still didn't think she could kick my ass . . . or at least my solar plexus. "Where's Clyde?"

"In Austin," Aimee replies with a skeptical look. "We agreed that, given the shifter-specific nature of magic you've run into, it makes no sense to bring a *Lossum* into the mix until we have a better idea of what we're dealing with."

Clyde is a Wild Card shifter, a Possum on his mom's

side and a Lion on his biological dad's. He can choose between the two forms at will. He may have agreed to take a wait-and-see attitude, but I doubt he'd sign off on her rushing solo to my side, regardless of the risks. "'Lossum'? Lossum sounds like a leaning flower." So she snuck away before dawn this morning without telling him. He'll be pissed. Eating with my fingers, I tear into the chops. "You could've let me know it was you, sent up a flare or something." I still feel guilty for tackling her.

"A flare?" she replies. "I was trying not to wake up the Morgans."

I'm confused again. "Who?"

"Kayla's parents." Aimee takes the bag, retrieves a set of plastic utensils and a napkin for me. "Here, you're making a mess. Her mom's a real-estate agent. And get this: her dad's the mayor. Seriously. The mayor."

"You're kidding!" I exclaim, noting that Aimee did her homework. "Is he insane?"

Werepeople have three options — live by ourselves on some remote chunk of earth, live in insulated all-shifter communities, or go mainstream and do our best to blend — something that comes a lot easier in urban than rural areas.

Taking a political job in a majority-human small town is two shades south of suicidal. Doing it as a parent is child endangerment.

International News Network

Transcript: April 19

Anchor: The *International Journal for Anthropological Discourse* reports that Dr. Uma Urbaniak, a University of New Mexico professor of prehistoric anthropology, has found the remains of a humanlike species that may have lived as recently as 2,000 years ago in Kazakhstan.

Dr. Urbaniak, some tabloids are reporting this discovery as the missing link. The television series *Cryptid Crazy* is featuring it as proof of the existence of yetis, a cousin to North America's own Sasquatch. What do—

Dr. Urbaniak: I'm of the opinion that what you see on-screen may be the partial remains of a previously undiscovered wereape in the midst of a shift. You'll note how the shape of the head mimics modern humans, but the arms are proportionally longer. Furthermore, we've never before seen a member of the *Homo* genus of such height. This man stood over seven feet tall!

Anchor: Are you sure he isn't the prehistoric equivalent of an NBA player?

Dr. Urbaniak: *(No response.)*

Anchor: So, you're saying that this proves the existence of wereapes. Do you think the species could have persisted into modern day?

Dr. Urbaniak: I didn't say it proved anything. But if this individual was a wereape and a representative one, I'd be surprised if wereapes still exist . . . unless they have significantly shrunk in stature or exist in utter isolation. These furry fellows would stand out from the crowd.

Anchor: And if they are a species of man, not animal or shifter?

Dr. Urbaniak: Then it's more likely that they fell victim to climatic change or, over generations, interbred with other werepeople or *Homo sapiens* until they were indistinguishable.

Anchor: Interbred? You heard it here first, ladies and gentlemen. Hybrids among us! Next thing you know, your grandchildren will be swinging from the trees!

(Dr. Urbaniak tosses her notes into the air and marches off camera.)

KAYLA

DESPITE YOSHI'S REASSURING TEXT, it's hard to sit still for breakfast. But I'm famished, and I'll probably need the energy. Besides, I don't want to make Dad suspicious.

My father is already dressed in period clothing—a top hat and three-piece silver-gray suit, complete with bow tie, shiny silver buttons, and pocket watch. Spiffy, but he'll be melting by noon. Dad sets a steaming stack of six pancakes in front of me.

Seated in my nightshirt and terry-cloth robe, I sneak a fingertip taste of the banana-walnut topping and maple syrup. Delicious.

"You didn't have to go to all this trouble," I say. "Especially since you're —"

"Better not to think about it," my father replies, referring to his diet. He's been low carb and low fat for two months and has lost only three pounds.

In contrast, my shifter metabolism means I could consume a baron of beef, a vat of cheesy broccoli macaroni, and a full pan of peanut-butter-fudge brownies every night without gaining weight — in fact, it's necessary for me to keep going.

After another moment at the stove, Dad joins me, his plate boasting only one pancake, and a whole-wheat naked one at that. "Dig in," he tells me.

Mom just left to meet clients in the nearby Tahitian Village Community (no, we're nowhere near Tahiti, and to make things even more confusing, the streets have Hawaiian names). Founders' Day weekend or not, Saturday is showtime for real-estate agents.

For a while, my father and I make chitchat about the local weather forecast. This weekend is critical to the downtown merchants and B&B/restaurant owners. It seems like Central Texas is always in a drought, but for the next couple of days, he's hoping not to get rain.

We always do this, have breakfast together. Dad calls it his most important meeting of the day. Sneaking Peso a piece of turkey bacon, he asks, "What are your weekend plans?"

"I . . ." I hate lying, but Jess already spotted me in town

with Yoshi last night. I'm pretty sure the werecoyote was a no-show, so we still have him to deal with, and especially given that the town's so crowded for the festivities, it's just a matter of time before someone mentions to my mayor-father that I've been seen with a nonlocal boy.

That boy himself is something of a mystery. Yoshi has zero Internet presence — I looked before turning in. If I say I know him from student government or running or UT's Engineering Summer Camp and Dad punches his name into a search engine . . .

Not that my parents don't trust me. I've never given them a reason not to, except for, fine, right now. I still don't want to reveal that Yoshi is a fellow Cat, either, not so soon after the Darby debacle, but also because that would be outing him to humans, which is a no-no, even if they are humans I love and trust.

What's more, I'm not ready to introduce him as a friend — we just met, and I'm not a hundred-percent sure I can trust *him* yet. Not with Mom and Dad.

"Something wrong, Kayla?" Dad asks, and I realize he's stopped eating.

I shake my head, offering a hopefully reassuring grin. "I thought I'd go out today and meet some new people. It'll be good practice for college."

Good practice for college? One reason I don't lie often is because I'm horrendous at it.

"Just be careful," my father replies. He reaches for the syrup, then, reconsidering, withdraws his hand. "If you catch so much as a glimpse of Darby — I mean, he's supposed to be leaving town, and he seems harmless enough, but —"

"You'll be the second to know," I promise. "After Sheriff Bigheart."

It's the right answer.

I wait until Dad departs for Founders' Day and then give it another five minutes for him to clear out of the neighborhood. Meanwhile, I book upstairs to my bedroom, Peso at my heels. I pull on a pair of shorts, tucking a copy of the spell into the front pocket, and a tank top that's a little lower-cut at the bust and higher-cut at the midriff than, strictly speaking, makes my father comfortable.

I'm not dressing for Yoshi. I'm dressing so that I can shift fast if I need to, and that works best without restrictive material binding my human form.

I may have given up on romance, but the thought of nakedness can be distracting. I doubt it'll come up, but if so, the whole transformation process works best starting naked, and that could mean naked me and naked Yoshi, if only to . . . What are we doing, anyway?

Oh, right. Tracking my Coyote stalker — focus, Kayla, focus.

❖ ❖ ❖

Taking stock of the clouds darkening overhead, I'm proud of myself for picking up the human girl's scent before I see her. I'm getting better at that. "Yoshi?"

"Come on up," he calls from my tree house.

Given the crash I heard earlier, I didn't expect to find Yoshi alone. But the newcomer doesn't look threatening. She has vanilla-blond hair with turquoise streaks, a small silver hoop through her left eyebrow, and tiny crosses tattooed around her pale neck. Yoshi introduces her as "Aimee," and he says her name like she means something to him.

They're seated, cross-legged, on my fuzzy throw rugs. She's fiddling with her phone, and he's flipping through one of my *Mechanical Engineering* magazines.

Her smile is welcoming. "Howdy."

Her tongue is pierced, too.

I wave, feeling small-town, clean-cut, and dull as cardboard.

"She's going to stand out," I say with a gesture. I'm not all that worried about it, but I need some way to explain my up-and-down stare.

Pushing to his feet, Yoshi laughs. "Please. Your dad waltzed out dressed like an undertaker." Yoshi waves the magazine. "Do you understand any of this stuff?"

"Of course." Not really, but I will someday.

Yoshi tosses the magazine aside. "I'm getting an A in phys ed."

Aimee snorts with laughter and still manages to be adorable.

I'm not sure what's so funny. "I take it Peter Villarreal didn't make an appearance?"

As Yoshi shakes his head, Aimee says, "He's pretty low-profile online, too, but I friend-requested him."

"Most shifters are," Yoshi puts in. "Low-profile, that is."

I'm not, and there's some subtext I'm not quite getting. Is he saying I'm a lousy wereperson? Maybe I don't know much about my shifter heritage or culture, but I refuse to believe that there's one right way to be a Cat or that he's better at it than me. Why is it important to Yoshi to be better at it than me, anyway? What does he have to prove?

Aimee leans forward. "Kayla, I read up on the guy, Benjamin Bloom, who died on the carousel. I'm sorry. I'm sure you grew up with him. But do you know anything about the history of the ride? Sometimes with magic attached to an object, a seemingly insignificant detail about it becomes important."

"Come again?" Yoshi says. "Where did you —"

Aimee swats him on the leg. "You said to research the mystical angle and . . . Kieren texted me the information."

"Kieren?" I hate being the odd-wereperson-out. "Who's Kieren?"

"Good friend of Aimee's." Yoshi makes a show of yawning. "Stuck-up, insecure Wolf-studies scholar, dating a hot redhead — also a good friend of Aimee's — who, incidentally, hates me (the Wolf, not the girl) and probably any other guy who dares to speak to his woman."

"How can anybody be stuck-up *and* insecure?" I want to know.

"Kieren doesn't hate you," Aimee replies in an exasperated tone, and I can tell they've had this conversation before. "Or 'any other guy.' But you shouldn't have ogled —"

"Ogled? I did *not* ogle. I was being friendly and —"

"Kieren said to call if we needed him," she puts in, as if that's the end of it.

"How big is Austin's shifter population?" I ask.

I've always read that our total U.S. population is estimated at something like one half of one percent, but there's nothing to say that the human sources typically quoted know what they're talking about, and it's in the best interests of shifters to lie.

Aimee's grin is wry. "Seems bigger every time I turn around. About the carousel?"

For a lot of reasons, I'm glad she's here, nudging me forward. As the mayor's daughter, I know more about the carousel than most. "The city council bought it from a traveling carnival that passed through town. There was a lot of talk about the fortune-teller, a Madame Zelda, who signed the papers, especially when she purchased retirement property adjacent to some acreage my parents own across the river. But no one ever saw her again. I think . . ."

"What?" Yoshi presses.

I meet his steady gaze. "She's . . . like us."

"She's a Cat?" he replies like it's no big deal.

Horrified, I check Aimee's reaction. She doesn't seem flustered. Then again, she doesn't seem the least bit fazed by relaxing in the company of two werepredators, either. It's stunning to think that the idea of what I am might seem like neutral news to anybody, that there are *Homo sapiens* out there, in addition to Mom and Dad, who're allies, friends, and maybe even more.

She's a better person than Ben was, that's for sure. Then again, maybe she's known about us her whole life. Maybe if Ben had had more of a chance to get used to the idea . . .

I remember him calling what I am a "nightmare." I remember him saying I was speaking for Satan when I tried to defend myself. Maybe he never would've changed, no matter what.

"It's okay," Yoshi says. "Aimee's cool."

Aimee extends her hand to me. "He's right," she says. "I am cool."

We shake. I have two sets of skin, and I'm nowhere as comfortable in either of them as she is in hers.

Seconds later, down in my backyard, Yoshi's rumbling stomach is audible. I can smell the remains of pork chops — Aimee must've brought him breakfast — but he's still hungry.

I could eat something else myself. I gesture, leading

them on. "This way. I'll give you a tour of quaint, historic Pine Ridge, or at least our culinary highlights."

"Damn tourists!" Miz Schmidt exclaims from the clotheslines straddling her backyard. "Can you believe it?" she asks us. "Somebody stole a pair of Dylan's jeans and his brand-new Spurs jersey. That cost me sixty bucks."

"The Coyote," Yoshi whispers next to me on the sidewalk, and I know he's right.

When it comes to backyard clotheslines, Peter normally would've had more selection on a Saturday, but only a few local housewives are willing to take their chances with the forecasted rain. "Sorry to hear that," I call. "I'll keep an eye out for the jersey in town." Put mildly.

"White with black lettering," Miz Schmidt tells me. "Number twenty-one."

"Got it," I say. "Hope your day gets better from here."

Founders' Day weekend features a cook-off, and the traditional categories are salsa and fajitas; chicken; pork; brisket; and chili. It'll be a while before any of the fancy stuff's ready to sample, but the festival food vendors should be up and running by now.

Aimee, Yoshi, and I stroll through the neighborhood past a long line of joggers and power walkers, all in dark-green T-shirts, participating in the Founders' Day 5K. I can already smell buttered popcorn, Elgin sausages, and turkey legs roasting from two blocks away.

As she passes, Brittney's mother calls, "There's our state champ, Kayla Morgan!"

The winded crowd cheers as they boogie on by.

Pine Ridge pride. I'm told the yearbook is dedicating a double-page spread to me.

"State champ?" Aimee asks.

"Cross-country. Track — hurdles and 1,600 meters." Lowering my voice, I add, "I take it easy on them."

"You're still cheating." Yoshi's tone is sharp. "And showing off."

What's his problem? I mean, sure, I have a certain genetic advantage, but it's not like I knew that when I fell in love with running. Some humans have more natural athletic ability than others, too, and they don't have to give up sports because of it. No, they win championships.

Yoshi adds, "The fact that you can outrun humans doesn't mean you can keep up with me."

I couldn't care less about keeping up with him. I'm about to say so when Aimee elbows him — hard — and rain starts to fall.

YOSHI

AFTER THE FIRST FLASH OF LIGHTNING, Kayla picks up the pace, veering from the booths and tents to lead us to the public library at the edge of downtown. Apparently, the festival will go on all weekend, rain or shine, but an electrical storm merits an intermission.

"Cute little town you've got here," I tell Kayla as I hold open the door for the girls.

She makes a show of rolling her eyes. "*That's* not condescending." When I don't take the bait, she adds, "Look, not everyone can afford to live in Austin or wants to. There's something to be said for caring about the people you pass on the street."

As we walk by the magazine display, Aimee stays out of it.

I press the issue. "Admit it," I challenge Kayla, winking at the librarian behind the checkout counter. "You're bored. You've been bored your whole life until now."

"What makes you think you know me?" she quips, leading us toward a gallery display of pastoral paintings (heavy on the wildflowers) by local artists. "We just met."

"I lived most of my life in the country," I admit. "But my grandmother's land was only twenty minutes outside of Wichita."

"Exciting," Kayla shoots back, turning at an overhead sign marked YA. "I'd rather live an hour *outside* of Austin than in *downtown* Wichita."

"Are you insulting Kansas?" I want to know. "Besides, I currently live —"

"That's enough!" Aimee exclaims. "Play nice, or I'll have to separate you."

We spend most of the morning waiting out the bad weather in the teen room, where I sit at a circular table, flipping through graphic novels while the girls visit, the two of them gazing, side by side, out the floor-to-ceiling window. Aimee's been chattering, making girl talk, mostly about Clyde, and using her phone to show photos of the two of them together. It's not like her to go on about him like that, at least not around me, but she's doing a good job of putting Kayla at ease.

"This is what we looked like after dominating the paintball range on Valentine's Day," Aimee says. "Are you going out with anyone, Kayla?"

Telling myself I'm not that interested in her reply, I sense a spike in anxiety, frustration, and something else — sadness — from the girl Cat. But her answer is curt.

"No." She adds, "I'm not a huge fan of Valentine's Day."

I sense a bad boyfriend. Aimee takes the hint and steers the conversation back to the weather. I'd rather hear about the fortune-teller, but this is a public place, and we don't need to broadcast our plans to all of Pine Ridge.

Given that the spell-caster guy, Benjamin Bloom, was killed by lightning, I don't blame Kayla or anyone else for taking cover (post-traumatic paranoia), but it's painful, waiting around.

"I see you've made new friends," a resonant male voice observes from the door.

Great. It's Kayla's father. Still dressed like an undertaker.

Apparently he didn't want to get rained on, either.

Eyes wide, Kayla spins to greet him. "Hi, Daddy."

Aimee grins. "How do you do, Mr. Mayor? I'm Aimee. I'm doing an oral report on small-town city governments for my U.S. government class. One of the chili teams referred me to your daughter and said she had the inside scoop."

Shaking her hand, Mayor Morgan says, "Kayla's picked up a lot from me over the years. But why would you be doing a report on city governments for a class on federal—"

"Extra credit," she clarifies, and I appreciate how smooth a liar she's become, practically as good as a shifter, and for most of the same reasons. Drawing out her phone again, she asks the mayor to pose for a photo, and he cheerfully obliges.

Before getting to know Aimee, I never thought much about the human allies and lovers of werepeople, let alone the human family members. But from his scent, Kayla's father is obviously in the latter group. He must be her stepfather, and it's her mom who's the Cat. Or maybe Kayla is part *Homo sapiens.* You can't tell by looking or by scent, not in human or animal form.

It occurs to me that he might've already been in office, or at least a professional politician, when he and Mrs. Morgan met. That would help explain his being in such a high-profile job now, despite his family's mixed-species makeup and the risks that come with it.

Even in twenty-first-century clothes, he'd be a distinguished-looking fellow—gray at the temples, a bit of middle-age girth around his belly. He's got a politician's charm and, unfortunately for us, the savvy to go with it. I only wish Aimee had come up with a cover story that had nothing to do with what he does for a living. It could be because I was raised without any, but I'm a big believer that parents mostly just get in the way.

"Interesting tattoo you've got around your neck," Mayor Morgan adds, as if on cue.

The repeating crosses. In Austin, nobody blinks twice at ink, but here . . .

"I'm a believer," Aimee says, steady and sincere. "I believe in salvation. I believe in true everlasting life."

She's not kidding. I'm not sure what religion Aimee is exactly, but she's not one of those vaguely "spiritual" people. She believes deeply in heaven, hell, and especially angels. She believes that Earth is some kind of battleground for celestial forces.

I don't make fun of it; not anymore.

"Good for you." Mayor Morgan looks chagrined. "Who's this?" he wants to know, turning his attention to me.

"Aimee's boyfriend, Yoshi," Kayla announces. "They're from Austin."

Right. Because an already-taken teenage boy is less threatening to the father of a teenage daughter than one on the prowl. (I've had my share of unpleasant interactions with fathers of teenage daughters — two of them involving firearms). I swing an arm around Aimee's shoulders and give her a quick kiss on the top of the head. "Nice to meet you, sir."

I hope Clyde finds out about this.

The sun breaks through the gray clouds not long after noon. We dash out to pick up a couple of roasted turkey legs for me and Kayla and a fluffy pink cotton candy for Aimee.

I'm impressed by how quickly the Founders' Day scene recovers. Bluegrass music rises from the performance stage. Restaurants and bars empty as festival-goers fill the streets, only to order more food and drinks outside.

We double back and take a winding concrete ramp down to park, positioning ourselves to cross the pea-green water. It's swollen and flowing at a brisk clip. The downpour has churned up a lot of debris. A bit of trash, vines, loose branches.

"This isn't good," Kayla mutters, tossing her turkey bone into a trash can. "We could take the highway bridge — there's a sidewalk — but by now Deputy Hoover has set up a roadblock to catch drunk drivers headed from the festival to the highway. He'll want to know where we're going and why, and he'll have a hissy fit if we take the historic bridge alongside it. It's a landmark, but a hazard. Half the town thinks it should be torn down."

Aimee frowns in the general direction of the bridge. "It's early in the day to be nailing intoxicated —"

"Klas's Kolachies opens for brunch at ten A.M. It's famous for its dollar-fifty home-brewed pints and dart games. I'm betting a fair number of husbands took refuge from the storm and their shopping spouses there."

Kayla is so plugged in. Her life's been completely different from mine. I merely existed at the outskirts of town in Kansas. I slip anonymously through Austin. I don't care like she does. I've never had a community that meant anything to me.

"We don't all have to go," I say as a blue heron takes flight from the water. "Aimee, you could wait —"

"Like hell," she replies, spraying her arms with insect repellent.

I knew she was going to say that. Still, the water looks dangerous for a human, and Aimee's got a wary expression on her face.

I pick her up in a matter-of-fact, rescue-worker kind of way. "Unless you'd rather ride on my back," I say, "consider me your first-class transportation."

The rising river isn't wide. After scanning the surrounding greenery, Kayla makes something of a game of leaping from the protruding top of one limestone outcropping to another. I wade, unwilling to risk dropping Aimee, but I'm still across in less than three minutes.

"Where does the fortune-teller live?" she asks as I set her on the muddy bank.

Kayla gestures southwest. "I think it's that way."

The Morgans' property is woodsy and dense. I can hear birds in the distance, but they become quiet when we approach, the way all birds do when cats creep by. Somewhere in the treetops, a sentry squirrel warns his kind that predators have entered their territory.

It's slow going with Aimee along. Not that she's out of shape, just that she's a human, not a Cat. I still can't believe Kayla thinks her state championships in track and cross-country mean anything. I could dominate in shifter high-school sports . . . if there was such a thing as a shifter high-school league. Maybe there will be someday, if the fanatics get their way and we end up living in total segregation. Not that I'm the type to dwell on political crap I can't change.

I'd much rather dwell on Aimee. She walks almost everywhere and is naturally high-energy. Plus she's taking tae kwon do two days a week. She's got a cute little figure, different from Kayla's. The Cat girl is all long, lean muscle with a tight round butt.

I'm not saying it's a competition. Truth is, there's pretty much no female body type that doesn't hold some appeal for me. . . . Still, I love a great ass.

"Clyde is half wereopossum, half werelion?" Kayla asks. "How is that possible?"

Stepping up and over a fallen tree, I reply, "Sometimes a Possum and a Lion love each other very, very much. . . ."

"Actually," Aimee puts in, "I think it was more of a strangers-in-the-night kind of thing that happened when his parents were separated. He didn't even know about his Lion heritage until this winter." Ducking beneath a branch, she adds, "They're nice people, the Gilberts —"

"I wasn't judging," Kayla replies. "I was realizing that, before this weekend, I hadn't thought much about other mixed families — shifter and human."

It's like she's been reading my mind. "Your dad is *Homo sapiens*," I say to Kayla, mostly so Aimee doesn't accidentally out me to the Morgans on the theory that they can already scent my Cat-ness.

Kayla extends her claws, more aggressively clearing the foliage. I do the same. Then Kayla says, "My mom is *Homo sapiens*, too."

"Uh . . ." I exchange a look with Aimee. "Are you sure it didn't just skip a generation?"

Not every wereperson is filled with shifter pride. Many pass as human, even in the most personal aspects of their lives, and some of those who identify as mixed human and shifter pray they don't pass on their animal forms to their children. I understand that. It's no doubt easier, less complicated, to lead a mono-form life. But the whole thing still pisses me off.

"I'm adopted," Kayla explains. "From Ethiopia."

In North America, it would be extraordinarily unusual for a Cat, or any shifter, to knowingly put his or her child up for adoption by humans, but maybe it's different overseas.

Aimee's brow crinkles. "Do you know anything about your birth family?"

"Before my first shift, I liked to think my biological parents were poor, desperate — that they wanted to give me a better future."

I can see where that would be more comforting than assuming that they're dead or just didn't want her. Ruby remembers our mom, but I don't even have that.

"I worried that maybe they had HIV or some other disease and couldn't afford medication," Kayla goes on. "Afterward, I wondered if maybe it was more complicated than that." She shakes her head. "My Cat form came as a surprise to my parents. To me, too."

By which she means her adoptive parents. Yeah, I bet they were surprised. I ask, "Any other shifters in Pine Ridge?"

"Just the fortune-teller," Kayla replies. "Not that we're close. I've never spoken to her."

I can't imagine what it must've been like for Kayla, growing up, alone and mystified by her very biology. Granted, Grams is far from nurturing, but I had my older sister, Ruby, too.

No matter what, the first few times you transform, it's scary, excruciating, and more than a little overwhelming. Accidents happen. Bystanders can get hurt.

It's rare, but young, unsupervised adolescent shifters have been known to accidentally kill themselves. And family pets.

That said, traipsing through the woodlands, I am

envious that the Cat girl has so much room to run wild in animal form. When I lived on Grams's farm in Kansas, I would occasionally shift under the cover of the wheat field, chasing mice or crows.

City living has caged me more than I like to admit.

KAYLA

"WHAT HAPPENED TO the barbed-wire fence?" Aimee asks, smacking mosquitoes as we push through the far border of my parents' property. I can hear a woodpecker hard at work.

"I cut it," I explain, steadying my new friend with a hand on her arm. "I cleared away as much of it as I could so the deer and other animals could escape."

"Escape what?" Yoshi asks.

In reply, I lift up a thick, leafy branch, clearing their view. "The fires."

The Austinites gape at the destruction. They no doubt saw news of the wildfires last fall, but up close, the scorched earth looks literally apocalyptic. We're faced with what appears to be an army of trees, upright but dead, charred halfway or higher up their trunks.

It's easier to pass through with the groundcover largely burned away, but it's more dangerous. "Listen for cracking, falling trees and limbs," I say. "It's not only the drought. The flames can burn all the way down through the roots, and the terrain . . ." As we continue through the rolling landscape, I add, "What with all the ash, it's not so stable, either."

I never risk crossing my parents' property line, so I'm surprised to see signs of recovery. As we continue on, I count three different kinds of what looks like sunflowers as well as tiny purple wildflowers and white ones resembling toy teacups.

"Pines in Central Texas?" Yoshi asks as we pass one that's been miraculously spared.

"Lost pines," I breathe. "People say they date back to the Ice Age."

He laughs. "They say the same thing about us shifters."

At the sound of splitting wood, I glance up and reach for Aimee. The branch is substantial and falling fast, but Yoshi leaps to intercept it, one-handed, before it can strike her.

That was a superhero-level move. As in Superman or Captain Marvel or Wonder Woman — not one of those billionaire types with tons of interpersonal drama and toys.

I've tested my speed and reflexes, but not my strength. Not like that. I've never really contemplated my full physical potential. Could *I* have caught that branch?

No wonder Yoshi scoffed at my state championships.

Suddenly, the fact that so many humans fear us seems more complicated than bigotry. They live farther down on the food chain. Throw in our intelligence, and certain species of shifters are apex predators. Werelions and Bears on land, wereorcas in the seas.

But smaller Cats . . . we're nothing to mess with, either. I wonder what it was like, between *Homo sapiens* and *Homo shifters,* in prehistoric times, before they somehow gained the upper hand. Did we make love or war? Did they hunt us, or did we hunt them? Just how bloody did it get? And how did we end up the losers?

To pass the time (or for my own good), Yoshi lectures me on the history of werecats and the controversy around whether we're distantly related to sabertooth tigers or at least sabertooth weretigers. He stops in place as if something occurred to him. "What about medical care?" he asks. "Did your parents ever take you to a human doctor?"

"Only for weigh-ins and growth measurements. I've had annual eye tests from the school nurse. My mom has issues when it comes to mandatory vaccinations." Extending my arms, I consider my health with a new appreciation. "I've never been seriously ill or broken any bones. Nothing like that. And once I . . ."

"Reached adolescence . . ." Aimee tactfully supplies.

Do all female shifters gain the ability to transform

shortly before the first time they start their periods? Is that something this human girl knows and I don't?

"Once that happened," I begin again, "there was no talk of taking me to a doctor." Or, to be specific, a gynecologist. I've wondered if young female werecats get a different version of the facts-of-life speech. I never dared to imagine what it might be like, being intimate with a Cat boy in animal form. Then again, I never met one before Yoshi, but here he is, hiking a mere five feet away, alongside me and his not-girlfriend. I swallow hard, thinking about it.

"You got lucky," Yoshi muses aloud. "Shifters tend to heal better than humans. We're immune to many of their diseases."

I already knew that. Embryonic human stem-cell research? Controversial. Embryonic shifter stem-cell research? Gaining steam with each passing day. Last week on INN, a doctor claimed we could be the ultimate game-changer; we could hold the secret to their immortality.

Yoshi adds, "I'm glad for you that your parents turned out to be so cool."

Me, too, but right now I've got more pressing things to worry about. Truth is, I'm not sure Madame Zelda stuck around after the fires. She may have packed up and left the area for good. A lot of people who lost homes last year did. A lot are still considering leaving.

My dad insisted that we go forward with the Founders'

Day weekend festival, despite the toll the destruction and drought have taken on Pine Ridge finances. It costs about a thousand dollars to remove a tree before it falls on someone's car or a house or a person. Roots untouched by flames can still die of thirst. Thinking it over, I'm personally grateful for what rain we've had, even if this weekend is supposed to be about attracting transplants and investors. Even if Dad is hoping it reminds the locals why they love the community so much.

As we come upon a large, tranquil pond, I spot the little log cabin built on stilts in the middle of the water, connected to the land by a curved wooden bridge with unfinished gray wood handrails. It looks unscathed, and the surrounding land is almost lush, dotted with wildflowers and wispy, lime-colored grass more than a foot tall.

A few steps more and I see the tail end of a small orange flatbed pickup truck, parked on a dirt road leading from the lake to who-knows-where in the forest. Probably the highway.

As I draw closer, the clouds above seem darker, denser. A large black bird, talons gripping, lands on a homemade sign nailed to the end of the bridge. It reads:

MADAME ZELDA
SPIRITUAL CONSULTANT
FIRST TWO MINUTES FREE

"How much do you think it is after the first two minutes?" Yoshi asks. "Then again, how much business do you think she gets out here in the middle of nowhere?"

"Maybe she put up the sign for our benefit," I say. "If she's really psychic, she'd know we were coming, right?" Twenty-four hours ago, I would've said I didn't believe in psychics, but given recent events, I'm willing to keep an open mind.

Aimee coughs. "If that bird says 'Nevermore,' I'm out of here." She's joking.

"If it says 'Nevermore,' we all are," Yoshi agrees. He's not.

The bird only squawks, but then distant thunder rumbles and a shower of rain chases us across the bridge. The only sign of life at the cabin is a fluffy, enormous, snow-beast-looking domestic cat sprawled, snoring, on a rocking chair beneath the overhang. He opens a lazy eye to regard us and yawns, stretching his front legs, as we walk by.

I have my hand fisted to knock on the painted green door when, without warning, it opens. Madame Zelda, I presume, is compactly built, with swirling gold hair — long for her age but it works on her, and her features have a stronger feline cast to them than mine or Yoshi's. Only the exoticness of her persona and occupation would allow her to pass for human.

At the sight of us, she sits straight down on the

wood-plank floor, pointing up at me with her mouth hanging open.

At first I think she's had a heart attack, but as I kneel at her side, she grabs my sleeve. "Whatever you're about to do, girl, wherever your young heart leads you, it could bring bloody and eternal ruin down on us all."

"I . . ." Sweet baby Jesus. I glance at my companions. "I don't know what she's talking about." Or do I? I think back to what I read on the National Council for Preserving Humanity website. The lunatics say we're everywhere, waiting for our moment to take over the world. They claim it's only a matter of time before a shifter is caught doing something so egregious that humanity will rise up to smite us. Yes, "smite." How often do you hear that in a sentence?

Has this older Cat woman foretold that I will somehow be the egregious one?

"Well, that was dramatic," Aimee puts in, bending to take Madame Zelda's other arm and help me half walk, half carry the fortune-teller to a chair.

"Time's wasting," Yoshi mutters. "She's trying to run out the two minutes."

The cabin looks to be a one-bedroom — sparse except for the gauzy, colorful scarves draped over a freestanding coatrack and the round table featuring cypress incense, white votive candles, and a small crystal ball on a matching stand. Presiding over the table, Madame Zelda glares at us. "Who are you and what are you bothering me about?"

I'm still unnerved by her earlier pronouncement. I'm a good girl, a straight-A student. I was Little Miss Pine Ridge at age five, with a sash, tiara, and everything. I've never brought ruin down on anyone. Except maybe Ben. Make that, *except Ben.*

After we give our names, Madame Zelda squints at Yoshi. "Any relation to Irena Kitahara?" She holds her hand up. "Stands about so high, likes to torture tiny trees, mean as snot?"

"My grandmother," he replies. "How do you know her?"

"First met at a Beatles concert in D.C. back in '64. Ran into her the following year at a voting-rights protest in Selma. It's been a Solstice-card relationship ever since." She flicks her gaze over his muscled body. "Irena never mentioned you were such a looker." Madame Zelda's open assessment of Yoshi is unabashedly sexual and more than a little icky, considering the age difference, though he seems to take it in stride. Mostly to herself, Madame Zelda adds, "She did say you were an idiot, though."

Yoshi smirks at that, and suddenly, I ache that he gets cut down so much at home. Does he have a safe place in the world? One where he can trust that everyone is on his side?

Aimee whispers to me, "You know that expression about it being a small world? Shrink it a thousand more times over, and you get a feel for shifter ties around the globe."

Shifter ties. Until now, I was a loose end.

Madame Zelda reaches to raise Aimee's chin with an insistent finger. "You've had some close calls, girl. You and your human soul."

"I can handle myself." Aimee jerks her chin away. "What's this about Kayla and ruin?"

"Humph." Madame Zelda slaps the top of the table, making the candle flames waiver. "Twenty dollars."

"Twenty bucks!" I exclaim. "For how long?"

"Five minutes," is the answer. "Seven. Depends on how long it takes me to get bored."

Yoshi's right; the woman is a professional con artist. We can't trust anything she says. Still, Aimee reaches into her pocket and extracts and presents a crumpled twenty.

Meanwhile, I take a closer look at my surroundings. The cabin is decorated with tacked-up carnival posters advertising MAN-EATING SNAKE, ALLIGATOR MAN, and BEARDED LADY.

I don't see a kitchenette or even a hot plate . . . or how Madame Zelda could have electricity. Maybe that's what all the candles are about.

"Have a seat, children," she says. "And call me Granny Z."

As we take chairs around the table, I default to my best manners. "Thank you for seeing us, Granny Z, ma'am. We're here to inquire about the carousel you sold to the town."

"You drink?" Granny Z stands. She moves to cover the windows with long scarves and then pulls a six-pack of beer out of a cabinet.

"No, ma'am," Aimee and I reply. I've never had an adult offer me alcohol before.

"I'll have one," Yoshi puts in with a half grin. He gestures to Aimee. "As you've noticed, this one is human." Then to me. "And this one plays by human rules."

I'm not sure if there's an insult in there, but Aimee doesn't seem to take it personally, so I decide not to, either. "Nice place you've got here," she says instead. "Very rustic."

"You're a city girl." Granny Z laughs, deep and throaty, and it feels like we've all come to some kind of understanding. "Not me. The road was my home for over fifty years." She serves Yoshi a Shiner Bock. Then she rejoins us at the table. "Ralphie, my late husband, rest his cantankerous soul, hand-carved that carousel, and for the animal figures, he chose the forms of shifters traveling with the carnival at the time."

"A remarkable piece of work," Aimee says, elbows on the table. "Say, um, was there anything unusual about the ride? You know, mystically speaking?"

Granny Z sets down her own beer with a thud. "What happened?"

As Yoshi fills her in on what we know so far, I retrieve the carefully folded copy of the spell Ben used from my shorts pocket and hand it over.

The fortune-teller studies it and starts cackling. "Oh, mercy, children! This isn't magic that humans can turn against us. The book this passage comes from is ours — *The Book of Lions, The Book of Old*. Benjamin Bloom was struck down for trying to use our faith against us." Granny Z bites her lower lip. "How on God's green earth did those NCPH bastards get ahold of this?"

Yoshi's eyes narrow. "Shifters are of the natural world. We don't indulge in demonic —"

"It's not demonic," Granny Z snarls. "It's not a curse. It's a blessing for healing. It's thought to *cure* grief, lunacy, even bona fide demonic possession. Not all magic is malevolent, boy. But right as rain, this invokes a higher power and it can be deadly in the wrong hands." She peers intently into the crystal ball in front of us and says, "Now, shush."

Seconds later, Granny Z's eyes close and she sways back and forth, trancelike, in her chair. For a while, we all try to decipher whatever it is that she sees in the shadows that flicker across the crystal. But we're left looking at each other, clueless about whether we should interrupt or leave her like that. Finally, Granny Z slumps forward.

"Is she dead?" I whisper, horrified.

"Of course she's not dead," Yoshi replies. "Can't you hear her heart beating?"

Excuse me, Mr. Cat, for not making a habit of listening in on other people's organ functions. Then again, maybe I should. I focus. "Yes, I can hear her heart beating."

"What if she's having a stroke?" Aimee suggests, pulling out her phone.

Granny Z bobs her head up and says, "Instead of the spell ripping the Cat out of you, it's bringing in shifters. The lightning strike, for lack of a better term, scrambled and superpowered it. I don't think it'll stop until you —"

"Destroy the carousel?" Yoshi asks. "How? Fire, chain saw? Does it matter?"

Granny Z shakes her head. "Only if you want to risk killing someone in the midst of being teleported in." To me, she adds, "What was this Benjamin Bloom to you?"

Here goes nothing. "Boyfriend," I finally admit out loud. "Newly ex-boyfriend, if you want to be technical about it."

Yoshi's brows rise at that — I should've told him earlier.

I try to keep the conversation moving. "You know what I don't get? The carousel has been broken up — the pieces separated and sold off. How is it that the various animal figures keep crossing paths with werepeople of those exact same animal forms?"

Granny Z turns to Yoshi. "Plays by human rules, you say?"

"Raised with a human sensibility," he explains.

Aimee tucks a strand of turquoise hair behind her ear. "Werepeople tend to seek out images of their animal form. I had a close friend who was killed, a werearmadillo named Travis, and afterward, shifter mourners brought plush toy armadillos as tributes to the spot where he died. It was sweet."

Okay, then. To Granny Z, I ask, "Any idea what we can do?"

She shrugs. "It's dangerous, but you could try to reverse it."

"What do you mean 'reverse'?" Aimee wants to know.

"Read the spell backward?" Yoshi guesses out loud.

"No!" Granny Z exclaims. "*Never* do that. I'm a fortune-teller, not a priestess, but with this particular blessing, I'd bet my last penny that the payoff is tied to the wielder's intent." She scratches her chin. "Replicate it as closely as possible. But with better intentions."

"Replicate it?" Yoshi repeats. "Do we need lightning?" His brow furls. "If that's what it'll take to pull off Operation Carousel, well, I don't happen have any in my back pocket."

"You need energy." Granny Z straightens in her chair. "But it'll come to you. Be ready for the ritual to rip it from the sky, if necessary. Be ready for the chaos to come."

Geriatric or no, she's quite the drama queen.

Without further elaborating, Granny Z stands and marches toward the bedroom. "Well, children, it's time I take my leave." She kicks a banged-up leather suitcase, covered with touristy bumper stickers, across the wood floor from the other side of the doorway. "Miss Kayla, you are welcome to come and go here as you please. Someday, you and your friends may need a hiding place. Someday soon."

I don't like the sound of that — any of it. "Wait," I say. "Where are you going?"

108

"Florida," she replies. "It's time. My granddaughter has taken over the family business. And . . ." She waves a letter at us. "Breaking news! The Old Alligator Man has proposed."

He's not a shifter. There's no such thing as a were-gator or, for that matter, a reptile-form shifter of any kind. The Old Alligator Man must be some kind of carny con or maybe he has an unfortunate skin condition, but none of the rest of us can resist glancing at the poster heralding her fiancé's unique appeal. Takes all kinds, I suppose.

"Congratulations," Aimee says, and Yoshi gives a curt wave good-bye.

I follow Granny Z out, leaving them talking in hushed tones. There's something I have to know. "If it weren't for the lightning," I begin, as the white house cat yawns up at us, "could Ben's spell have worked? Given it was his intent, could he have turned me into a human being?"

Thundering across the bridge, she replies, "Is that what you want? To be a *Homo sapiens*?"

When I don't reply, Granny Z steps onto land, tosses her beat-up leather suitcase in the cab of the orange truck, wrenches open the rusty door, and climbs into the driver's seat. "The Alligator Man's proposal isn't the only reason I'm skedaddling out of these parts, and you — especially you — might do the same."

She slams the door shut and adds through the rolled-down window, "Meanwhile, take care of Junior for me. He has a touch of the sight, but he's just learning how to channel it. And I don't have the heart to do to him what should be done."

She's talking in riddles. I ask, "Who's Junior?"

With a cough and a sputter, the truck starts up and she drives away.

As I return to the cabin, a furry white humanoid head rises from the pond with a fish between its teeth. The creature drops the flopping fish on the bridge and hauls himself up.

His dripping, all-white coat likewise covers his entire body — he's definitely a boy, though it's probably not so obvious when his fur is dry. He stands about my height and, kicking his catch back into the water, he slowly blinks at me with large ice-blue eyes.

In a guttural voice, he says, "Junior is me."

YOSHI

I'M IN NO WAY HAPPY TO SEE, as a friend of mine liked to put it, a goddamned greedy yeti trail in, soaking wet, behind Kayla. It smells literally fishy, but it lumbers toward me with a goofy grin and asks, "Are you both werecats, too? I am a cat person. Not a *Cat*-person, obviously, but, you know, I love cats. I even have a cat, Blizzard. You probably met him outside."

"Yoshi is a werecat," Kayla informs it. "Aimee is a human being."

At the same time, I exclaim, "Where did you find *that*?"

It babbles on, "Did you know that most of the big wild-cat — not werecat, *animal* cat — populations are shrinking at an alarming rate? Experts blame loss of habitat, trade in body parts and pelts, a decrease in —"

"*His* name is Junior." Kayla crosses her arms. "He's alone in the world. Yoshi —"

I growl. "You can't trust anything it —"

Aimee holds up a hand. "Enough." She disappears into the bedroom and comes back with a beach towel. Tossing it to Junior, she asks, "Has Madame Zelda been raising you?"

As he dries off, the yeti clarifies, "Was, and before her Jennie, the bearded lady. Well, them and the rest of the carnies. Granny Z warned me that" — he makes air quotes — "'the sun was setting on our time together.'" Realizing he's still dripping on the wood-plank floor, he drops the towel and stands on it. "I can't take the Florida humidity — the Texas heat is bad enough. And I'm not alone. I have Blizzard."

Blizzard? Oh, right, the house cat. Forgive me if I'm not charmed.

This winter Aimee, Clyde, and I were kidnapped by yetis — they refer to themselves as *Homo deific,* which means "God people" (the egomaniacs) — and brought to a remote, private tropical island, called Daemon Island, in the Pacific, where she was forced into servitude, he was caged, and I became big game for high-dollar hunters (half

112

of them supernaturally demonic and soulless and all of them out to kill me for my animal-form pelt and trophy head). We barely escaped alive, and put mildly, I'm not a fan of yetis as a direct result of that experience.

"Granny Z said we should take care of him," Kayla tells us. "And I guess Blizzard, too." Glancing at the yeti, she asks, "Um, what kind of shifter are you?"

"He's not one of us," I spit out, heading for the door. "He's the enemy."

Junior recoils, and I feel a flash of guilt.

"He's a person," Aimee says, blowing out the candles. "Like humans and shifters are all people, just from different branches on the evolutionary family tree."

Technically, she's right. The yetis — they're not really yetis; I just call them that — are naturally born, but they're even deeper in hiding than we are. Their species is single-form, so they're more closely related to humans. They live in total secret, originally in the Arctic and now around the globe, manipulating worldwide financial and political systems with the aid of mega money, tech, and human flunkies. Plus, they're known to dabble in demonic magic. Did I mention how much I hate magic? "We should get out of here." I point. "But not him."

"He was *raised* by a shifter," Aimee reminds me. "How old are you, Junior?"

"Thirteen or so; I'm not sure. I was abandoned at the carnival as a baby."

What was he, a sideshow act? "We could turn him over to our favorite Austin police detectives," I suggest, "and expose the international crime syndicate that is —"

"Don't talk crazy," Aimee says. "We're taking him home with us."

"Oh, for God's sake," I exclaim, tossing my hands up. "He's not a puppy!"

Junior opens his mouth as if to protest, too, but Kayla cuts him off. "*My* home?" she asks, as if Aimee's lost her mind.

Because the scorched forest is perilous and Junior needs to watch his step, Aimee insisted that I carry Blizzard. Given that he can smell that I'm a werecat, my feline passenger is alternating between ducking his head in the crook of my elbow and glowering at me. I've been bitten twice — skin broken and bleeding. Tiny claws are buried in my forearm. I don't mind, though. He may be a very, very distant cousin, but he's still family. Unlike Junior.

"I am not letting that cat pick on Peso," Kayla announces. "And what exactly do y'all expect me to tell my parents —"

"It'll be okay," Aimee says. "I have a friend, a priest, who's great about stuff like this. He's based outside of Chicago, but if I call, I'm sure he'll drive down as soon as possible. Junior is not our problem." She favors him with a reassuring smile. "The spell is."

"What spell?" Junior adds, brightening.

"Isn't that confidential?" I demand. "You haven't even known him for an hour."

"Yet." Kayla nudges, "Aimee, why don't you call your priest friend now?"

Aimee is silent a moment. "I'll wait until I have more privacy." Her voice doesn't betray it, but I know her well enough to tell she's pissed at both of us. At me for not giving Junior a chance and at Kayla for clinging to her unrealistic expectation of having a completely average, humanlike life.

"Who's Peso?" Junior asks, skirting a fallen trunk.

"Her dog," I explain. "She's a *dog* person."

I'm sure Aimee's right that I overreacted. Now that I know Junior's alone and a big kid, I don't so much care about him one way or the other, except that we have to figure out what to do with him until Father Ramos —

As the earth folds, crumbling, under me, I tumble, tossing Blizzard toward Kayla, frantically grabbing for tree roots that tear away, burnt to nothingness.

"Yoshi!" Junior shouts from above. "You okay?"

I dig my claws into the side of the ashy pit and keep sliding. "Stay back!"

Lunging, I seize a thick root that holds, catch my breath, and begin my painstaking climb back up. "I'm good!" I yell. "Give me a few minutes."

It's a tough climb — a foot gained here, two lost there. I have time to think about what Granny Z said about replicating the spell. We'll have to track down the stored, shipped, and/or purchased figures and come up with a way to return them to the carousel . . . while recreating as closely as possible the ritual itself, including the time, place, and atmospheric conditions.

We'll need a dark and stormy night, at the very least.

I can hear the others talking above.

"Do you need help?" Junior wants to know, because naturally it's the smelly yeti who cares and neither of the irresistibly cute girls.

"Stay back!" He's built thick and already as tall as I am. I bet he clocks in at well over two hundred pounds. I don't need his giant yeti feet caving in more land around me.

"You seem awfully concerned with Yoshi," Aimee observes, knowing full well I can hear her. "And after he was so rude to you."

"He's a Cat!" Junior reminds her. "Cats can be prickly, and it takes a while to win them over. You have to be patient with them and continue offering feathered toys and tasty treats."

"We are not animals!" Kayla exclaims. "Wait. Is that why you were in the lake, trying to find us a treat?" She pauses. "Then why'd you throw the fish back in?"

"I'm so sorry!" he replies. "Did you want it?"

And so it goes for the three or four additional minutes it takes me to crawl to the surface and reunite with the others. Junior promptly hands Blizzard back to me.

My patience shot, I fume. It seems like the least he could do is transport his own pet.

"Is there a point to this?" I say as tiny claws re-embed themselves. "In case you missed it, I've already fallen once, and —"

"And Blizzard is fine!" Junior shouts, bouncing in place. "You saved him."

The yeti blinks at me with grateful blue eyes. God!

As we continue on our way, Kayla glances sideways at me. "What's this about a *Book of Lions*?" she asks.

"*The Book of Lions, The Book of Old.*"

Aimee interjects. "Is that one book or two?"

"One," Junior puts in, "but it goes by both names."

It's disturbing that he's the one who knows that. I admit, "I'm not the religious type, but it's obviously associated with a werelion faith."

"A spell book?" Kayla counters.

Aimee sounds almost prim as she replies, "An angel would say there are many paths to the Big Boss. Maybe it's archaic, pagan. Like people who worship Zeus. And Granny Z said the text wasn't a spell or a curse. It's a blessing for healing."

Kayla coughs. "Forgive me if I'm not feeling blessed."

"Wherever its history, we have to deal with the here and now," I point out. "If we don't want the carousel figures to keep fetching shifters, we'll have to round them up and keep them out of circulation. Step one of Operation Carousel: Track them down."

Aimee nods. "If we're going to replicate the spell as closely as possible, we'll need them to reassemble the ride."

She beat me to saying so. I turn to Kayla, "So Ben was your boyfriend?" It explains . . . I'm not sure what it explains exactly, but it's personal to her, very personal and relevant as hell, given the circumstances surrounding the spell.

"I'm sorry for your loss," Aimee puts in, her tone warning me to tread lightly.

I don't. "How did Ben find out you're a Cat, anyway?"

Kayla bites her luscious lower lip. "I told him."

"Rule number one for our kind," I say. "You can't trust humans."

"Hello?" Aimee pipes up. "Walking right beside you through the dead forest."

"*Most* humans," I amend. "You have to be more careful and stop keeping secrets."

"Keep secrets, don't keep secrets," Kayla counters. "You're contradicting yourself." She sets her hands on curvy hips. "Don't tell me—"

"Are you friends?" Junior asks. "You don't talk to each other like friends."

That shuts everybody up. We walk in silence the rest of the way to the border of the Morgans' property, mercifully without plunging into the ground again or being crushed by a falling tree.

We're finally at the river's muddy edge when Kayla wants to know, "Is it true your grandma is as mean as snot?"

"Worse," I admit, glancing down. "Oh."

The water is higher, faster, break dancing over the rocks.

I hand off the white cat to Kayla, preparing to carry Aimee.

I doubt Junior can swim any better than a human, probably worse, what with all that fur to weigh him down. But he's not my priority.

"No, no, don't be stupid." Kayla squints toward the highway bridge. "Beats me how we're going to explain ourselves to Deputy Hoover, but we're taking the long way home."

Right then Blizzard sinks his teeth into her arm and, dropping him, she hisses and loses her balance, teetering on a rock drenched in rising water.

"Whoa!" Kayla tumbles backward into the drink with a splash and a yelp.

"Kayla!" I jump in after her, but the water is muddy, cloudy. Popping my head up, I shout, "Where'd she go?"

"I don't know!" Aimee exclaims, scanning the rapids.

Werecats are known for our speed, strength, and grace, but we can't hold our breath any longer than humans and we're not naturally great swimmers (with the exception of Tigers).

I dive back under, gripping roots for support. I can't see a damn thing.

How long has it been? Did Kayla suck in air before

submerging? How long does it take to drown? So much debris — branches, leaves, trash. This is impossible. I can't . . . There's not . . .

Underneath in the murk, something big and fast-moving flips past my leg.

What the hell?

I rise until my vision is clear of the water again, and, glancing over my shoulder, I see a brown furred head surface. A split second later, Kayla, coughing hard, rises alongside it.

Make that *him*. Wereotter. Male. In partial shift.

Fighting the current, I wade after the Otter and Kayla to the park side of the river.

"We're taking the long way," Aimee shouts from the bank bordering the forest. "We'll say we walked from a hotel along the highway."

Right, because without Kayla, she's just another tourist. It's not a bad story — simple, plausible. Except for Junior. But I have enormous faith in Aimee's creativity in a pinch. Besides, once you say you're from Austin, other Texans expect some weirdness from you. Along the tree-and-scrub line behind her, I notice that Junior has retrieved Blizzard from a branch.

Aimee waves. I wave. "Be careful," I yell. "Stay sharp."

Junior may be only a goofy kid, but to me, "yeti" still equals "danger." I hate letting them out of my sight. Still, I can't leave Kayla. She throws up water as the Otter retracts his shift. Her hands have been cut on the rocks. There's a tiny bleeding gash across her cheek. But the Cat girl will heal fast. All shifters do. Finally, she wipes her mouth with the back of her hand.

"Your shirt?" the Otter prompts me.

Right, because he's naked — we're talking full frontal and backside exposed. Only a few yards away is public parkland. Even with the stormy weather, anyone from the festival might wander this way. I peel my shirt off, toss it at him, and ask Kayla, "You all right?"

She stands and wrings muddy water out of her clothes. "All right enough."

Once he's in nearly human form, though still furry, the Otter's able to get my shirt over his head. He's short enough that it falls almost to his knees. "Evan," he says. "I'm Evan."

Evan is trim but soft-bellied and has spiky light-brown hair.

I ask, "Where are you from?"

"Bartlesville, Oklahoma." He points to the carousel. "Somehow I got over there." Which is enough of a mystery that you'd think it'd occupy his full attention.

Instead, he takes three swift steps to Kayla, reaches for her arm, catching her off-balance, and bends her back in a passionate clinch.

It's a move I've considered once or twice myself, big with the romantic drama, but not right after the girl in question has nearly drowned and vomited.

KAYLA

WHEN I REGISTER EVAN'S TONGUE slipping into my mouth, I jerk back and flip him hard over my shoulder. Behind me, Yoshi laughs as the Otter flies into the murky river with a splash.

Undaunted, he lunges back up, bobbing in the tumultuous water. "I must have you! I must taste your every crevice and —"

"Evan!" Yoshi shouts. "There will be no crevice tasting. Wake up and smell the eye of newt. You're bewitched!"

"Bewitched, besotted, all I am, sweet lady Cat, is burning for your love."

Somebody flunked his Shakespeare unit.

Hyperaware of my revealing wet top, I hold up my hand in warning. "I don't care if he might've saved my life. I cannot deal with this."

When I run in Cat form, I always wait to shift until I'm on the forest side of the water, deep inside the cover of the brush and trees. It's like entering another world — dark, private, safe. But the river doesn't seem like much of a welcome mat anymore, at least not when it's trying to kill me. After several tedious moments, Yoshi — alas, no longer shirtless — returns from escorting the Otter to retrieve his stashed clothes. Was it only last night that we searched this same patch of woods for Peter's? Nakedness has never before been such a pressing concern in my life.

Yoshi announces, "I warned him that if he touched you again —"

"I can take care of myself," I insist as Aimee and Junior come into view, far downriver. I realize the fact that Evan rescued me negates my point, but I dare Yoshi to challenge me on it.

"I know," the Cat replies with a tight grin. "I told him you'd shred his junk like a scratching post."

I did not need that mental image. "Where did Evan go?" I ask, wandering alongside Yoshi toward the paved path.

"I pointed him up toward the festival to get some chow."

Fair enough, but I don't like the way Yoshi's studying me. "What?"

"You sent Darby the Deer home?" he asks, like I haven't already said so.

I sink onto the metal park bench. "My parents did. What were we supposed to do, keep him?" When Yoshi doesn't reply, I add, "Why? What difference does it make?"

"He's enchanted, and you're responsible for him."

"And for Evan? And Peter? And you?" I exclaim. "I didn't ask for this to happen."

"You're a Cat, and you shared that information with a human—"

"Who's dead because of it. I loved Ben. Don't you understand that? How is it that I haven't been punished enough?" I don't need this right now. I get up and jog away from Yoshi to meet Aimee and Junior and his cat. Keeping me in sight, Yoshi lets me go.

Sure, it's *fine* to tell Aimee what you are. She's *fine* with it. She'll rush to help you with your shifter-related, fatal mystical crisis, whereas Ben . . . caused it.

Moments later, I'm blinking back tears as Aimee greets me with, "What did Yoshi do?"

"It's nothing," I say. "I'm fine. Everything's fine."

"You're too fond of that word," Aimee observes.

It's impossible to skirt the festival without being seen. It's spilled over into the neighborhood. People are everywhere. Yoshi and I are still drying out and look a little river-battered. Cuts. Scrapes. My hair is a disaster.

"Well, what do we have here?" Sheriff Bigheart wants to know, giving Junior a friendly slap on the shoulder. "Aren't you hot in that getup, son?"

"I'm with the snow-cone people," he replies in a cheerful voice. "I came early to help set up, but they're caught in traffic behind a wreck on Highway Seventy-One."

"There's a wreck on Seventy-One?" is the reply. "I haven't heard anything about that."

It occurs to me that a cop won't swallow any old story and has the means to fact-check it. "Are you sure it was Seventy-One?" I ask. Offering my best A-student grin, I explain, "He's not from around here."

"Uh-huh." Pulling his phone out, the sheriff gives us a vague wave and moseys off. "Stay out of trouble, Kayla." His voice deepens in warning. "You and your new friends."

Yoshi points at Junior. "Let me or Aimee handle any future cover stories."

He leaves me out of it. Apparently, I'm not smart enough to finesse my own hometown.

We find a nervous-looking Evan, drinking Dr Pepper out of a can and nibbling on beer-batter-fried fish on a stick. He looks fine. Only his hair is still damp. He makes no eye contact and angles his body away from me, even if he is sneaking glances at my butt and boobs. I'll have to remember to thank Yoshi later for coming up with such an effective threat.

125

"Is there a dunking tank?" five-year-old Joey Bratton asks, eyeing me as he skips by.

"A filthy one?" asks Mrs. Bratton, handing him a bright red balloon.

Never mind that I'm all cut up and in the company of a head-to-toe furry kid. People are fine with that. My being wet, dirty, and in the company of strangers, including strange boys?

Fascinating.

I gesture toward a side street and lead the others behind Betty's Baubles, which deals in all manner of rhinestone jewelry and cowgirl clothing but is best known for its jalapeño jam. "This isn't going to work," I announce. "I can bring Aimee home, maybe Yoshi. But Junior is —"

"We could go back to Granny Z's," Junior points out, snuggling his cat. "Me and Blizzard and Yoshi and Evan." He strikes a rapperlike pose. "Boyz in the house."

It's not a bad idea. She did say we'd need the cabin and were welcome to it. It never occurred to me to leave Junior there alone, but I'm not about to introduce Evan to my parents, either. He may be a pervert only because he's enchanted, but he's still a pervert.

"What about Peter?" Yoshi asks.

My instincts are telling me he's never far. I swallow hard. "What about him?"

Yoshi replies, "He's unstable, dangerous —"

"I can be dangerous, too." I take a step and rise on my toes so we're nose to nose.

As Yoshi laughs — laughs — at me, the others take a giant step back. "Listen, kitten, you've got the equipment" — Speaking of perverts, is that a leer? — "but you don't know what to do with it." Somehow I get the feeling he's not just talking about my teeth and claws.

"Time out." Aimee shoves herself in between us and stares up at him. "You go to the cabin with Evan and Junior." Addressing the Otter, she asks, "Do you have a phone?" At the shake of his head, Aimee withdraws hers and hands it to Yoshi. "You'll probably need this. I bet my phone is the only one that wasn't drowned. We'll call you later."

"Do I get a say in this?" Evan wants to know.

"No!" comes the answer from everyone but Junior.

Evan reaches for the dry phone. "I have to call my —"

Yoshi holds it away from him. "And tell your *whoever* what, exactly? You can't mention the spell, and you can't leave town until we get this all sorted out."

"Who put you in charge?" Evan asks, puffing up.

Yoshi lets out a low warning rumble, and Evan seems to shrink inside his own skin. The male Cat's not in charge, but there's some kind of pecking order between different types of shifters. I'm grateful to be a predator species.

Not that Aimee, a petite human girl, seems the least bit intimidated. "Hopefully, we'll have this cracked in no time," she tells Evan in a soothing voice. "And between now and then, we can come up with a plausible explanation for your disappearance. I hate having to do that to your family, but right now you have to trust me when I say it's necessary for your safety and ours."

I can tell Yoshi doesn't appreciate being dismissed. If he were in Cat form, his ears would be flat against his head, but he pivots, leading the other two guys away.

Aimee's word carries a lot of weight.

As they trail after Yoshi, Junior claps the Otter on the back. "You can say you ran away to join a traveling carnival! We'll call you Otter Boy. I even know some carnies who'll vouch for you."

The drying mud on my skin makes it feel itchy. Ditto the scrapes where my skin has already begun to knit. Passing what was once Ben's house, I say to Aimee, "You're not afraid."

"Of what?" she asks, glancing around the historic neighborhood.

"Me, Yoshi, Evan, your boyfriend, Clyde," I reply. "Werepeople in general."

"From what you and Yoshi have said, I'm not a fan of that Peter guy, at least not so long as he's in a mystical state."

"Mutual," I reply. "But that's about his *behavior*, not his species."

Aimee's smile is slight, almost apologetic. "It's not

like I'm joining hands and protesting down the streets of Birmingham or even starting up an 'I Like Shifters' page on —"

"No," I reply. "You're loving people as individuals. You're loyal to them, you sacrifice for them, and not to score political points or to congratulate yourself on your sensitivity."

It occurs to me that I could be friends with her for real. We're already moving in that direction, and it's not like with Jess Bigheart or practically everyone else in the world. I don't have to risk that she'll reject me based solely on what I am. I already know she accepts me.

I don't have to worry that revealing my secret will place her in any more danger than she's already placed herself in.

"Thanks," Aimee says, blushing. "Let me guess. You scored high verbal on your SATs."

"I did better on . . . why?"

This time the smile reaches her eyes. "Call it a hunch."

I pick up my mail on the way into the house. One letter doesn't have a stamp on it or, for that matter, an address: just my name. "I don't recognize the handwriting."

"Hmm." Aimee sinks to her knees, greeting the yelping Peso. "Hey, little guy!"

Meanwhile, I open the envelope in the foyer. "It's Peter," I announce. "He dropped by while we were out." I hand her the letter. "And left this." The note reads:

Don't underestimate the danger you're in.
I will come for you when the moment is right.

It's signed with a Coyote paw print.

Aimee studies the words and the mark on the paper. "There are scarier things in the world than a lone teenage werecoyote, but that doesn't mean we should underestimate him."

I snatch the note away. "Call Yoshi on my parents' landline in the kitchen. Tell him to come back to the house. I'm going to brush, rinse, and take a very long, very hot shower. Maybe two."

YOSHI

"LEAVE YOUR SHOES ON THE STEP," Kayla orders at the back
door, about a half hour after Aimee called to summon me
to protect them. Not that she put it in those words.

I don't admit what a relief that was. Or how much my
ego appreciated it.

Kayla adds, "No mud on my mother's rugs. Laundry
and bathrooms are upstairs. Do *not* use the shower in the
master suite; use the one off the hall. Once you're clean,
look in my dad's wardrobe for an old bathrobe. Do *not*
touch anything else in my parents' room. Until you're
clean, don't touch anything else — period." When I roll my
eyes at Aimee over her shoulder, Kayla says, "Go on. You're
nothing to look at and smell worse."

"Are you sure it's okay to leave Junior with Evan?" Aimee asks. "We barely know him."

"We barely know Junior," I point out, shucking my shoes off. "Besides, Evan's an Otter. A randy one, but they're known for their upbeat temperament."

At her raised brow, I add, "Look, I'm not trying to stereotype. 'Chipper Otters' and all that. But he was decent company on the hike back to the cabin, though he did wax poetic about . . ." I try not to let my gaze fall to Kayla's chest, but she catches me looking. "Your, uh, assets." Smooth, Kitahara, very smooth. "There's fresh water, plenty of food in the cabin cupboards, and fish in the pond. They'll be fine until Father Ramos arrives to fetch Junior."

"Speaking of which," Aimee says, putting her hand out, "my phone?"

I return it to her, and she excuses herself to make the call.

By the time I return in Mayor Morgan's frayed robe, the girls have raided the refrigerator for snacks. The microwave beeps. Aimee pulls out a ceramic bowl of steaming *queso* and sets it next to serving baskets of blue tortilla chips, veggie potato chips, and kettle corn.

Right now Aimee's is our only personal phone that works, though the girls have slipped mine and Kayla's into a zippered plastic bag filled with white rice in hopes that it'll draw out the water. I'm not optimistic that it's going to work. Lifting the bag, I shake the rice around like I'm breading chicken. "At least my phone was cheap. I can pick up a new —"

Kayla slams a hefty beef sausage onto a plate, cracking the ceramic, and then gasps at what she's done. Aimee purses her lips, and though I don't read people as well as she does, I can smell the frustration and anxiety coming off Kayla. She's not quite at her wit's end, but she doesn't know her own strength. It visibly shocks her back to her previously composed self.

Kayla holds up one finger, takes a deep breath, and prompts, "Aimee?"

Straightening in a kitchen chair, Aimee reports, "Father Ramos is leaving Chicago after he 'puts out a few fires.' He hopes to pull in here tomorrow night around ten-ish, depending on traffic. He'll call when he hits town limits."

"That's one problem solved." Kayla hands me the note from Peter. "Technically, it helps that the shifters being teleported by the carousel are drawn to me —"

I scan it.

"Except that we aren't all friendly," I say, finishing the note. Son of a bitch — what a psychopath. I sniff the piece of paper. It carries the faint scent of Coyote and cheesy fried chicken. Peter has been at the fest downtown. He's walking the streets, not cowering, Coyote-style, in the shadows. He's confident and unashamed.

I set the note on the table beside the popcorn. It's

written on the back of a deposit slip in blue ball-point ink. Now we know Peter stopped by the First National Bank of Pine Ridge, which means he's probably been video recorded.

Given this documentation and the number of pics of Kayla on his phone, it wouldn't be hard to prove he's been stalking her. Still, that could draw unwelcome attention (and too many questions) to us as well, so I file that away as a plan of last resort. I never thought I'd consider turning a fellow wereperson over to human law enforcement, but if that's what it takes to protect Kayla, I'll do it.

Aimee asks, "What about the carousel figures? How could we track them down?"

As I circle around to the counter and pluck a knife from the cutlery holder, Kayla swings into the chair beside Aimee's. The Cat girl says, "The Stubblefield sisters promised to resell them outside of Bastrop County."

"Stubblefield," I echo, moving to slice the sausage. "That name sounds familiar."

"Sassy older ladies, sisters . . . They own Stubblefield's Secrets on Main," Kayla informs me. "It's the two-story storefront across from the cotton-candy booth, the one with the antique birdcage on the sidewalk."

Still carving the sausage, I say, "What with their Old West design, the carousel figures are fairly unique items. Can I borrow your computer?"

"In my bedroom," she replies. "The password is CalTech1891."

I'm sure she'll change it later. But I should have a few minutes to poke around.

The ornately carved staircase groans as I jog up to Kayla's room. Within seconds, I've booted her laptop and logged on. I do a main file search of "Benjamin Bloom" and pull up dozens of photos. Whenever Ben's not looking at the camera, he's looking at Kayla.

Every humanoid species — Tasmanian weredevils, yetis, *Homo sapiens* — has its own variation of body language (though we werepeople are reared to mimic the latter's). The way he's smiling, touching her arm, his eyes . . . I can almost see why Kayla trusted him with her secret. Poor kid. When their relationship went south, it must've felt like a meteor hit.

My instincts tell me he never meant for all this to happen. He never meant to put her in danger. However screwed up in the head, Ben loved her. On some level, she knows that.

It must make all of this so much harder.

I click to open the browser's search history, highlight, and delete.

KAYLA

"I'M SORRY ABOUT YOUR BOYFRIEND," Aimee says again. "I mean, your ex-boyfriend."

"I'm fine," I repeat. I don't know these people. I owe them because it's my fault Yoshi's here and Evan, too, and Darby in Fort Worth and even Peter, wherever he might be, and of course Aimee came on Yoshi's account. But I don't owe them the whole truth of Ben and me.

I'm not sure I even know the whole truth of Ben and me.

I just have to stop what's happening.

I have to put an end to the misdirected spell, blessing, *whatever* and its effects, for good.

Peso's scratching frantically to go outside. "I'll take him," Aimee announces, diffusing the silence. She gets up, snags the leash hanging from a hook, attaches it to his rhinestone collar, and exits the house. I turn to apologize to her — for I'm not sure what — when the door closes behind them.

Yoshi thunders downstairs with my laptop to work alongside me. Why did I give him my password? Oh, well, there's nothing that interesting on my hard drive anyway, and I guess I needed a break, a few moments without him hovering. So much for that idea.

"Where's Aimee?" he asks.

When I tell him, Yoshi peeks out the window at them and says they're playing fetch. It's a good call. Peso's got energy to burn, and being cooped up in the house isn't helping.

"Brace yourself, kitten," Yoshi says, cracking his knuckles. "I've got some real-world skills to put to work here."

I favor him with a half-smile. "Congratulations. You've mastered the search engine."

Yoshi's a wonder on the antique sites, though, pulling up a carousel snake figure in Corpus Christi, a bear in Houston, both bighorn sheep in Oklahoma City, a wolf and both ponies (plus their wagon) in Dallas, Darby's deer in Fort Worth, Evan's otter in Bartlesville and its mate in Waco, Peter's coyote in Fredericksburg and its mate in San

Antonio, and Yoshi's own cat at his grandmother's antiques mall in Austin.

I'm not sure about skills, but he's definitely got real-world know-how.

"I used to volunteer regularly at the animal shelter," I say, embarrassed by my compulsion to puff myself up a bit. "But my scent freaked out the dogs and rodents."

Yoshi lifts an eyebrow. "So, you're not all about machines. You like warm-bodied creatures, too?"

Flirt.

Finally, he announces, "We're still missing one deer, one snake, a bear, a wolf, and both hares, buffaloes, elk, hogs, raccoons, and armadillos — basically the animals that humans find less sexy."

I have no idea what he finds so funny. "As animals go, I'm pretty sure wolves are considered sexy." Even if it is disloyal to my species to say so. "There's a cat missing, too," I add. The one that represents me, the one Ben used to cast the spell in the first place.

"Is it possible the unaccounted-for figures haven't sold yet?" Yoshi asks, dipping a sausage slice into the warm, spicy cheese.

"They're not on the display floor at the sisters' store." If the figures were for sale at Stubblefield's, I would've heard about it.

"Is there a back room?" he suggests. "Or attic storage?"

"Attic," I suppose. "It's a two-story building."

He drums his fingers on the table. "I'm in the business. I can say Grams is interested in buying for our shop and asked me to swing by and take a look. We can buy them."

"Aren't you forgetting something?" I tap the screen. At his blank look, I add, "The moola. What are you, made of money? The carousel figures are all priced at over a thousand dollars. The ponies are nine grand!"

"Well, they are in good shape," he replies. "Ponies are popular, and we're talking Dallas. You'd never get that much for them—"

"It doesn't matter!" I exclaim. "We don't have that kind of—"

"What about your parents?" he replies, wandering to the window to check on Aimee and Peso again. "What do they know about Ben's spell?"

I drop my tortilla chip. "They're devout Christians. They would completely freak out if I told them he'd dabbled—"

"The type of Christians who believe all shifters should be burned at the stake?" Yoshi wants to know. "Yourself exempted, of course."

I push up out of the chair. "No, the type of Christians who do unto others as they would be done unto, but not incidentally would also do *anything* to protect their only child from any connection to maleficent and destructive magic."

"You don't have to tell them the spell part," Yoshi counters, sauntering toward me.

"Then how would we explain . . ." I begin as Aimee strolls in and releases Peso from the leash. I add, "Never mind. My parents aren't rich."

"You could fit my grams's entire apartment in the front half of your house," he replies.

"Enough already!" I counter. "My mother is a real-estate agent. Of course we have a great house."

"Oh," he says. It's nice to have shut him up.

Ignoring us, Aimee moves to the laptop and clicks through the open windows showcasing the animal-shaped carousel figures. "So we need deep pockets and discreet drivers. I'll take Yoshi's car and head to Austin to round up help. You two check on the local antiques shop; see what they still have in stock here. Once we've got all the figures, we'll reassemble the carousel and reverse the spell."

She makes it sound like no big deal.

She and Yoshi are either cockeyed optimists or nuts.

"What're you going to do?" I exclaim. "Rob a bank?"

"No," she says, matter-of-factly. "I'm going to explain the situation to a couple of my friends who're crazy rich, supernatural savvy, and love me more than s'mores. If they say no, then we'll have to steal the carousel figures, but I seriously doubt it'll come to that."

"Steal?" I echo. "What do you mean —?"

"Kayla," she says, getting up in my face, "we are talking

140

about enchanted antiques. Malevolent magic. If we have to get clearance from heaven above to justify protecting the unsuspecting wereperson population from them, I will make that happen. Understood?"

"I—"

Yoshi snaps his fingers. "Don't involve any shifters whose animal forms—"

"Are represented on the carousel." She blows her bangs off her forehead. "Obviously."

I hate feeling like the weak link. "Aimee," I begin in a softer tone, "is there a way to warn the shifter population? Put the word out that the enchanted carousel figures are out there and should be avoided or at least dealt with on a strictly hands-off basis?"

She and Yoshi exchange a long look, like they're communicating telepathically. "Maybe," Aimee replies. "I'll see what I can do."

YOSHI

AFTER AIMEE TAKES OFF in my car, I pull on my still-damp clothes and hike downtown with Kayla. "The shifter community in Austin must be tight-knit," the Cat girl says.

"I'm still fairly new in town," I admit. "Through Clyde, Aimee is a lot more plugged in than I am. Plus, she has friends at work. They will give her the money, no worries."

"What?" Kayla asks. "What work? She can't *tell* people. . . . Who?"

"Relax." I laugh. "Aimee knows who to trust. She washes dishes at a vampire-themed Italian restaurant called Sanguini's. It's this Goth cosplay hot spot, and the food is —"

"I've heard of it," Kayla admits. "Wasn't someone killed there?"

I nod. "The original chef. The owner and the current chef both have heaping bags of cash, and they adore Aimee. They'd do anything for her. If she says she can get funds and drivers, she can get funds and drivers. She's awesome that way."

" 'She's awesome that way,' " Kayla echoes. "And you're just friends."

"Aimee is dating Clyde," I reply.

"I can tell you're thrilled for them," Kayla replies, too smug.

Before Aimee, girls were strictly for sexy fun time, a bit of stolen recreation in Grams's barn loft or the backseat of my car. Kayla is the first shifter girl of my own age that I've really hung out with. It makes sense that she's more perceptive than most human girls would be, even a sensitive one. Kayla can literally scent out my emotions.

It's taking some getting used to, but I have no choice with her but to be real.

As we weave through the festival crowd on Main, I'm struck by how people here say "Howdy" as you pass them on the sidewalk. Unlike in Austin, folks in Pine Ridge talk the way I'd expected of Texans before moving down. You hear "y'all" in Austin, even "all y'all," but hardly any vowels that go on for two beats. It's the difference between "I'm going to the store" and "I'm go-o-in' to the store" or, to be more exact "I'm go-o-in' on down to the store." To be completely honest, I didn't expect to see African Americans in small-town Texas, either, but so far I've noticed maybe a dozen black folks (besides the Morgans) since I hit Pine Ridge.

I also can't help noticing the row of U.S. and Texas flags flying from every storefront. There was a time when werepeople were notorious for draft dodging — fearful of being outed by the medical exam. But before DNA testing caught up to us, shifters served under General George Washington, fought on both sides of the American Civil War, collaborated with the French underground during World War II.

No doubt there's a lunatic or two in this town who'd want to see me swing from the trees if they discovered the truth about my heritage. But if a foreign power threatened, I'd still do whatever I could to protect Pine Ridge and, for that matter, Austin and Butler County, Kansas. The fact that you're being persecuted by your own nation doesn't mean that you can't be a patriot. Or that other countries aren't worse.

"We'll need something that belonged to Ben," I say. "A tangible object." I don't mention the incantation, what with so many people around, but she knows what I'm getting at. We need to bring all the spell ingredients together, not just reassemble the ride itself.

I've never had an honest-to-God, big-time, double-capital-*R* Romantic Relationship, so I've never had any of the material crap that comes with them. But Aimee's always forgetting her backpack in Clyde's car, he's always giving her this or that to put in her purse, and before my sister, Ruby, moved out, I discovered one of her girlfriend's double-D purple lace bras hanging over the shower door (which is way sexier than finding a bra that belongs to your sister herself or, worse, your grams). Relationships come with stuff.

"I don't have anything." Kayla's forehead puckers. "I burned it all."

At least I can gauge her emotions as well as she can mine. When Ben's name comes up, the main thing I'm getting off her is anger and more than a twinge of regret. Stages of grief and all that. "Don't worry," I say. "I'll think of something."

"Don't you mean *we'll* think of something?" Kayla steps closer, speaking so low that only a shifter could hear. "His locker was emptied the week after he died. His mother has packed up and left town." She releases a long breath. "What about Ben's original copy of the spell? I might be able to get it from my friend Jess."

I shake my head. "We're looking for something more personal."

She rubs her eyelids. "Nope, burned it all."

"Woman scorned, huh?" I reply, trying to jar something useful out of her.

She chooses to ignore that. Pointing over my shoulder at the storefront, Kayla says, "I can't go in there with you and act like the carousel pieces mean nothing to me. I was Ben's girl. I signed the petition demanding it be disassembled. I'm supposed to be traumatized."

Supposed to be?

Glancing at her sports watch, Kayla adds, "It's almost six, the shop is closed Sundays, and we can't afford to wait until Monday morning. The storm system will have moved east by then."

Throwing an arm around her, I guide Kayla to a sidewalk bench. "You know these Stubblefield sisters, and you've spent a little time with me. Can I charm my way into their storage area, or should we come back later tonight and risk breaking in?"

Touching the lady Cat may have been a mistake. I'm hyperaware of her body heat, and the feeling seems to be mutual. Her honey-brown gaze locks onto mine, and however strong she's fighting it, with a little more privacy and a lot less overriding drama, I'm almost sure I could talk Kayla out of her Levi's. Almost.

Without blinking, she replies, "Let's try your charm first."

"What's your secret? What's your secret?" The parrot whistles in his vintage brass cage as I stroll past it, baring my teeth.

146

Grams would dismiss Stubblefield's Secrets as a foo-foo shop, stocked with clichéd reproductions and rehabbed antique furniture for the shabby-chic and organic, hand-painted upholstery crowds. Peacock feathers punctuate sparkly gold urns, cherub figurines perch on silver-flecked black-granite-and-ironworks tables, and polished cobalt-blue toy marbles mimic water in shiny brass bird fountains. The mini TV on the counter is tuned to ESPN.

A plump calico house cat—a store cat—lounges on an armoire, chewing on the remains of a feather. I watch an equally plump little kid (I'm guessing age three or four), holding a giant swirly orange-and-white lollipop, approach the cat and reach with sticky fingers for her tail.

The cat hisses once, ears back, meaning it, but the kid and his mother, who's trying on vintage straw hats, pay her no mind. The pudgy little hand inches up again, and, turning so no one can see my face, I hiss simultaneously with the calico, magnifying the sound.

The brat recoils, bursting into tears, but the calico graces me with a look of approval.

We understand each other, she and I. She knows biting or scratching a child would jeopardize her meal ticket, but someday she's going to shred and devour the annoying, chatty parrot in the antique cage positioned outside the front door. It's just a matter of time.

The place reeks of potpourri and warm scented

oils — apple, cinnamon, and citrus. My eyes are watering from the stench. I hate potpourri. It should be outlawed.

No, even worse than that are the princessy old dolls displayed in lacy pink-and-white baby clothes. I hate their freakish, staring painted/plastic/glass fake baby eyes. I hate the way they're lined up on the high shelves, toys kept out of the reach of children.

That said, the dolls obviously are the store's signature items, and if you log on to the shop website, they're what's featured on the home page. On the next shelf down, more are posed, most of them designed and decked out to mimic little girls.

"Nice selection," I say as an attractive seventy-something woman wearing vintage rhinestone cat-eye glasses bustles by. "But that Madame Alexander Cissy is a tad pricey considering that her ring is missing, don't you think?" I don't fit the typical dealer profile, so the posturing is all about street cred.

Her clicking heels stop short on the bronze-colored concrete floor. She looks me up and down and says, "Are you one of those fancy boys?"

I think she means gay. On average, humans tend to be way more uptight about sexual orientation than shifters. When my sister came out to Grams, the only comment over fried steak and mashed potatoes was "So long as you're happy and she's a werecat . . ."

I wonder if my grandmother would approve of

straight-A Kayla, even if I was the one to bring her home. She'd have to. Kayla's perfect — smart, pretty, smart — nearly annoyingly so.

God, that's a tempting thought. Kayla could hold her own against Grams's barbs or totally disarm her with the über-polite good-girl, small-town chitchat. It's practically a super weapon against adults. If we survive this, I may have to go for it.

"My family's in the trade," I explain, fishing a damp Austin Antiques card out of my wallet and handing it over.

The shopkeeper tilts her hair-spray-shellacked head up at the shelf. "And you can see that her tiny doll ring is missing?"

Oops. I've been so busy showing off my antiques savvy that I forgot to camouflage my inner Cat. "My name's Yoshi." I unleash the smile. "I'm in town, visiting a friend — a Miss Kayla Morgan — so I thought I'd stop by and say howdy. My grams and me, we're new, doing business in Texas —"

"Well, isn't that nice? I'm Lula, and you're a friend of our dear, sweet Kayla?"

Bigger grin, no matter that she reeks of vanilla rose fragrance. "I am. I thought she could use some cheering up, and . . ."

A woman who looks so much like Lula that she must be her sister (and stinks just as badly) is wrestling a huge, ornate, gold-framed beveled mirror from behind the counter.

I'm moving before it starts to slip and grab it with both hands before it shatters against the concrete floor. "Here you go. Safe and sound."

Jackpot. I'm their hero. The customer who bought the piece is happy with me, too. Lula introduces me to her grateful sister, Eleanor, as I help them slip the mirror-frame corners into cardboard sleeves and wrap it up in thick brown paper.

"Kayla told me about Ben and what happened at the carousel," I say once we've got the package loaded onto the buyer's flatbed and secured with rope in an alley behind the store. "Tragic," I'm quick to add.

"Yes, tragic," Lula echoes.

"Poor Kayla," Eleanor adds. "Her first love, and they were precious together."

Precious. "You bought the carousel figures?" I say.

"No, no," Lula assures me, holding open the back door.

As the wind blows in behind us, I cough, nearly choking on the ladies' floral perfume.

Eleanor comes back inside, too, offering Coca-Cola in chilled Mexican glass bottles to a couple of women wearing T-shirts that read TIME TO WINE. Then she explains, "We agreed to handle the sales as a favor to Constance Bloom, Ben's mother, and the city council. A shame they decided to break up the ride. It added so much to the town's character."

She studies her manicured nails. "Anyway, the money is being used to offset the expense of the memorial installation in the park — cost a fortune. I told Mayor Morgan not to hire those pretentious artsy people from Dallas."

"Were the animal figures hard to unload?" I ask. "What with the economy and all . . ."

"You weren't friends with Ben?" Lula asks. "Just Kayla?"

"Just Kayla," I say, hoping they hadn't been inseparable for so long that Lula wonders how that's possible. "I thought maybe my grams could take a few of the carousel figures off your hands."

Brightening at the prospect, Lula leads me up a steep, narrow staircase, decorated on either side with silk holiday wreaths, each dolled up with a fake, sparkly bird and big red velvet bow. They're tacky and a noticeable quality point beneath the rest of the goods on display. "Local artist," she whispers in a confiding tone. "Minister's wife. Personal favor."

Ah. There's a sign on the attic door that reads PRIVATE, but it isn't locked. There must not be much crime here in Pine Ridge, or it could be that people are that trusting.

I follow Lula into the attic, and there they are: one deer, one snake, a bear, a wolf, and both hares, buffaloes, elk, hogs, raccoons, and armadillos. We're golden!

No, wait, the other cat is still missing.

Which means it's already sold, and any associated web listing has probably been already taken down. Not good. I'm pretty sure we need the whole set. "Austinites will go gaga over these babies," I say, weaving between the massive elk and stout dillos. "The whole Old West carnival theme has great regional appeal, and they've got that spooky vibe, to boot. Top-notch conversation pieces." I make a show of bending to more closely examine the merchandise. "Some wear here and there . . ." I'd normally work harder to bargain her down, but it's not my family's money I'll be spending, and Pine Ridge could use the cash infusion. "On the knees, ears, chins, and tails, but that adds to the rustic appeal."

"Exactly what I've been saying," Lula agrees with a clap of her hands.

"Did you unload any of them to locals?" I almost swing up to sit on a buffalo before remembering that I'm supposed to be acting professional. "I get where that might be awkward, what with what happened, but these are unique, fairly irresistible to the right buyers."

"Locals?" Lula echoes. "Nope, like you say, awkward."

She smells like she's lying. "Kayla mentioned something about Ben bringing her photo with him the night he died. She seemed upset about it, but it's only natural he'd carry a pic of his girlfriend in his wallet. I wish I understood what went down so I could help her through it better." Could've been smoother, but that's my best shot.

I give it a moment. Two. No dice.

At least I tried. "Well, I can't speak for Grams, but I'll tell her —"

"Kayla's photo was taped to one of the carousel cats," Lula blurts. She moves to shut the attic door. "Eleanor and I were the ones who found his body, you know."

"No!" I say, pretend-shocked. "I had no idea. How awful for you both."

She nods. "We think something horrible and satanic was going on."

Finally. Thank you. "Was Ben the horrible and satanic type?" Because I could seriously use some intel that didn't come from his button-down and grieving ex-girlfriend.

"No, no," Lula assures me, pulling white drop cloths off a few other stored pieces for me to peruse. Freestanding brass lamps and coat hangers, a rocking chair, antique Victorian porcelain knickknacks. "Ben and Kayla both . . . wonderful kids, the crème de la crème of Pine Ridge. Churchgoing, good grades, athletic, and they had the sweetest young love. Everyone knew it. Never mind that he was white and she was black. Nobody said 'boo' about that."

Nobody? Lula just mentioned it herself.

Humans can be petty and baffling. When your body can shift into animal form, I guarantee that obsessing over little things like the color it is in human form seems awfully ridiculous. Then again, there are age-old feuds among shifters, too. Cats and Wolves, for example. Orcas and Tusked Dolphins.

153

She goes on, "Constance—Ben's mama—she had him buried in the necklace that Kayla had given him for Valentine's Day. It had a gemstone on it, a gold cat's-eye gemstone."

"Valentine's Day?" I echo, pretending to examine some uneven paint (a bad patch job) on the ear of one of the hare figures.

"He died the very next night," Lula reminds me. "Broke that darling girl's heart."

That darling girl. I haven't gotten that off Kayla, that kind of sorrow. She could be blocking it. Shifters are better at that than humans. It's tied up in what Grams so poetically calls "the inheritance of the wild," a gift of our animal forms.

In the battle for survival, you don't have time to indulge every emotion, which in no way means that sooner or later, whatever you're pushing down won't explode.

KAYLA

I'VE COMPLIMENTED AT LEAST two dozen people on their outfits (lace and ruffles are all the rage with the older ladies) or their children (several of whom have had their faces painted — a couple to look like cats), asked every passerby carrying a bag what they bought (printer's-drawer miniatures are popular), and taken a thorough survey of public opinion on the festival cuisine. An Austin-based winery offering free tastings is moving product by the case, and the Davis Family barbecue pork ribs are to die for.

I'd have already snagged a rack for myself, but I don't want to abandon my post. While making small talk and waiting for Yoshi, I've been scanning to no avail for the werecoyote.

Wait. Is that . . . ? Yes, I catch a glimpse of reddish hair, Peter's wiry frame, and his long face. He's barefoot but wearing Dylan Schmidt's stolen San Antonio Spurs jersey and jeans. The Coyote's intense gaze locks onto mine, and there's something too intimate about it.

I catch my breath for a moment, frozen in place. He shakes loose of the connection before I can, ducking behind a group of boisterous Bubbas in matching patch-covered leather vests and jeans.

I'm up like a shot, but they're big men, a half dozen of them, belly laughing at who-knows-what. A couple of new moms pushing baby carriages block me to one side, and a great-grandma shuffling along with the aid of a walker cuts me off on the other.

"Excuse me, excuse me," I say, my manners so well programmed that I feel guilty for being rude and weaving between them, even though Peter is . . . nowhere to be found.

Where did he go? I turn all the way around, studying the crowd. He's not at the booth selling Native American and cowboy art or the booth selling handmade pottery or the craft tent for kids or standing in line to use a port-o-john. He couldn't have gotten far.

I cross the street to scale the back side of a bald cypress. I make every effort not to be spotted in the branches, but the crowd is already distracted by the historical society board members parading down the sidewalk in head-to-toe steampunk, complete with parasols, bustle skirts, aviator goggles, and leather vests and bustiers. I'm very sure Pine Ridge's actual founders never looked so magnificently coiffed. It's all quite the spectacle.

Dad was hoping to top last year's record of 3,500 in attendance, and I bet we're way past that. But there's no Peter to be found.

Dejected, I return to wait for Yoshi as he finally emerges outside the antiques shop. Lula gives him a grandmotherly peck good-bye, licks her thumb to clean her signature rose-plum lipstick off his cheek, and then scoots the parrot cage inside to lock up for the day.

Thank God. That bird's incessant chatter was getting on my very last nerve.

Pretending like I don't *notice*-notice Yoshi is making me all itchy.

He slides on the bench, stretching his muscled arm behind me. Not resting on my shoulders, but the body language is possessive. A few passing sophomore girls, volleyball players, pause to stare and whisper. Or maybe they're just marveling at his radiating sexiness.

He has good news — all of the carousel figures, except one, are accounted for. "I'll ask the sisters about the cat figure when I come back to purchase the others."

With Aimee's buckets of money. I report my brief Peter sighting — at least I think it was him. "I have no idea where he could've skulked off to," I conclude.

"Hmm, Coyotes are skittish by nature, but . . ." Yoshi's hand falls on my shoulder, and my skin tingles beneath his touch. "Where would you normally be this weekend?"

It's a rhetorical question. I stand, leading Yoshi deeper into Founders' Day.

At the booth with hand-dipped candles, Bitsy Metula is collecting signatures for a petition to forbid werepeople from working in private or public day-care facilities. You know, like the one shifter in this whole town — that would be me — even wants to be a professional babysitter. Talk about pointless posturing. I don't stop to see which locals signed the sheet. I don't want to know.

After polishing off two racks of pork ribs respectively, Yoshi and I split an Almond Joy pie and wash it all down with lemonades. It's refreshing not to have to pick at my food like I normally do at school or did with Ben. Yoshi doesn't think twice about my appetite.

The Cat takes my empty plate from me and tosses it — a small thing, but Ben would've expected me to clean up after him. Not that I should be comparing them. So I'll stop. Now.

"Let's take the festival systematically," Yoshi suggests, "street by street, table by table, booth by booth, and ask around." He pivots toward the dunking booth. "Hopefully, somebody's seen Peter. Talked to him."

He's insane. "I can't just walk around town asking

about some strange boy with . . . some other strange boy."
I hate the way it sounds, like I care too much what people
think. But I can tell Yoshi doesn't get it. He's not the First
Daughter of Pine Ridge.

"I'm not that strange, and you've already been seen
with me." Yoshi pulls Peter's wallet from his back pocket.
"We'll say we found this." He opens it up, showing me
the driver's license in the clear sleeve. "Look, photo and
everything."

Despite his whole man-of-action attitude toward
Operation Carousel, Yoshi lingers at Jim Doyle's display
of artifacts found over the decades along the river. The old
buttons and bullet shells, a gold pocket watch. Yoshi may be
the last to admit it, but I suspect he secretly enjoys working
at his grandmother's antiques mall. I suspect he's great at
it. Maybe he'll never win any academic awards or graduate
from a fancy college. But he's in no way stupid, and he's better with people than I'll ever be. No wonder he's so good at
sweet-talking women.

We don't have any luck until the Adopt-a-Friend booth.
"I remember this boy," Lisa says, stroking a whining mutt
puppy. "He came by yesterday after you took off for dinner.
He asked about Floppy, said he'd always wanted a pet rabbit. But there was something about his eyes I didn't like."

I'm glad Lisa listened to her instincts. I've felt the call
of the hunt in animal form, but I'd never . . . "Did he mention where he was staying in town?" I ask.

Lisa sets down the panting dog. "You might turn that wallet in to Sheriff Bigheart."

We pushed too hard. "Great idea," Yoshi agrees. "Kayla, let's go find the sheriff."

It's getting late. The streetlights and festival lights on the music stage have been turned on. "Let's take a break," Yoshi says, gesturing to the miniature train.

We choose the "caboose" bench, three back from the next nearest passengers. The O'Donnell quadruplets (forty-something parents, fertility drugs), they're in second grade now and making a huge racket. But that means Yoshi and I can talk without being overheard.

"If we're going to reverse the spell," he begins, "we'll need *something* that belonged to Ben. Do you have any ideas at all?"

I've been thinking about it. "Coach Reiss retired Ben's football jersey. It's hanging in the school hallway, alongside the trophy case." It's been sheer hell, having to pass by it every day on the way to gym class. I can close my eyes and almost see him, owning the field.

"Do you care about the jersey?" Yoshi asks. "Does it connect the two of you?"

I shake my head. It's blasphemy to say so in Texas, but I find football incredibly boring. I've always attended all the games, but that's because everybody's there. It's a social thing, a community obligation. My parents go to network, and of course, dating Ben, I was expected to be cheering him on in the bleachers. I like baseball better, and in point of fact, Ben was better at baseball, but it's not nearly as big a deal culturally.

"Lula mentioned something about your giving Ben a necklace," Yoshi says as the train chugs around the bend in front of city hall.

"For Valentine's Day." It comes flooding back. The hours of babysitting to make the money, shopping the Web for just the right pendant, the way I hid the flat little white box between my mattresses and rehearsed in my bedroom mirror what I was going to say . . . only to completely blow it, to lose everything. Lose Ben.

Mrs. Bloom had him buried in it as a gesture to me, I think, to what he and I shared.

He'll wear it forever. The present from me that ultimately triggered his death.

Yoshi is quiet. He doesn't touch me. He doesn't move. He whispers, "I'm sorry."

"'Sorry' doesn't change anything," I say. "'Sorry' doesn't make Ben less dead."

"That's not . . ." Yoshi takes an audible breath. "I mean, I'm sorry we'll have to steal it."

"*Steal* it?" What is he talking about? Why are he and Aimee so obsessed with thievery?

The train stops, and he whispers, "We need to break into Ben's casket, take that necklace, and use it to try to reverse the spell."

"That . . . That's ungodly disrespectful!" I exclaim. "You—"

"So is what's happened to me and Evan and Darby and Peter," Yoshi replies. "For all we know, the werecoyote was a sweetheart of a guy before your boyfriend's spell got ahold of him. I am sorry for your loss, Kayla, and I'm sorry that this is necessary. But it's not just about you."

KAYLA

WHEN I SET THAT GOLD CAT'S-EYE gemstone in the center of Ben's palm, the single furthest thing from my mind was that, in the not too distant future, I'd have to rip it off his dead body.

The only other option I can think of, though, is to call Ben's mother and try to somehow explain why I need something that belongs to him that's significant to both of us, especially when I had so much of ours and torched it all. No, no matter how terrible it may be . . .

Ben won't mind. He's in heaven.

At least I hope he's in heaven. Using magic — shifter or otherwise — has to be a sin, but Ben was a Christian and Jesus forgives. Jesus is all about forgiving.

On the plus side, Yoshi talked to Aimee. Operation Carousel has cash flow and liftoff.

It's past 2 A.M. on Sunday, God's day, and here I am on the edge of town in the middle of Dogwood Trails Cemetery, standing outside of Ben's family crypt.

It hits me how far the Blooms — cotton farmers, originally — go back in Pine Ridge history, how hard it must be for Ben's mom to start over. But then, she's only a Bloom by marriage. Maybe after losing her husband and son, to her this land feels more cursed than consecrated.

After shimmying out my bedroom window and down the honeysuckle trellis, I managed to pull some tools out of the garage, along with old sheets to wrap them in, and Yoshi stuffed it all in his backpack.

I've barely said a dozen words to him since our conversation on the miniature train. He's respected my silence, and I appreciate that. I hate what we're about to do.

"No security?" Yoshi finally asks, and I hear the relief in his voice.

"This is Pine Ridge," I reply. "Most people don't bother to lock their doors."

He probably thinks I'm angry with him. It's more complicated than that. Since Ben died, until Darby showed up, it was like I'd been sleepwalking. This weekend has been such a twisty emotional mix — scary and confusing, but at least I feel more alive again. I don't want to be like this. I don't want to need these boys to reclaim my whole self.

Maybe, though, it's not about them. Maybe it's just that the animals in them call to what's primal inside me, and without that, I've been letting my head get in my way. As usual. I overthink everything. I'm out of touch with my own nature. With nature itself.

The cloud cover mutes the moon, shadows the stars, but my Cat eyes can see anyway. I focus on the velvet of the night, the wildflowers that dot the grass-and-clover cemetery grounds. Bluebonnets, Indian paintbrushes, and prickly pear cacti, all a backdrop to more crypts, upright marble markers engraved with Texas stars or roses. A smattering of U.S. flags, one Confederate. Asshole. The trees bloom purple, like beautiful bruises.

I used to love spring.

"Why don't you wait out here?" Yoshi says. He extends a claw to pick the lock, then retracts it. "The lock's been broken," he whispers. "Keep watch."

I hear a rusty creak as he opens the door. Yoshi smears Vicks under his nose before pulling on thick garden gloves. I force myself not to think about why.

"No, wait," I say, reaching for the Vicks. "I can't let you do this for me."

Even with our heightened vision, the inside of the stone crypt is deathly dark, and it's all I can do not to gag at the mint-menthol smell of the medication. How many Blooms are entombed in here, anyway? I brush my hand against a bouquet of . . . daisies, I think . . . that have been laid across Ben's father's casket. Mrs. Bloom must've left them here before leaving town.

I'm surprised to discover she didn't leave flowers to remember Ben, too, but I have more pressing matters to worry about. I slide the backpack off Yoshi and unzip it.

Ben was buried in a hardwood casket, so after doing some online research, we brought pliers and screwdrivers to use on the thumb locks. A crowbar in case the lid has been nailed down. I fumble it, and metal clangs on concrete, too loud and scolding.

"My fingers are tingling," I whisper, testing them against each other. "It feels like all the air went away." I glance at the door, still open a crack. "Did all the air go away?"

"Easy, kitten," Yoshi says, bending to pick up the crowbar. "Why don't you wait outside? It'll be over in a minute or two. Then we can set everything right and move on with our lives."

He sounds sure of himself. It's tempting to let him handle it. Yoshi may not be totally objective, but he's not remembering what it felt like to sway in Ben's arms at the Homecoming dance. He doesn't know what it felt like to have Ben's warm lips linger at my ear.

"Did you hear that?" the Cat adds, raising his nose. "From outside?"

I didn't. Then I do. A thick, heavy foot (paw?), much bigger than a Coyote's, crushes straw covering a fresh grave. I know exactly where it is. Mr. Cruz died two weeks ago of a heart attack. He was a cheerfully grizzled man in his nineties, worked as a greeter at Wal-Mart for thirty-five years after a career in long-haul trucking. His death was sad but not shocking, which isn't to say that anybody local would tromp all over his resting place.

Well, maybe a couple of the defensive linemen, if they were drunk.

But they don't smell like . . . what *is* that scent?

I hear something like a huffing snort, and the fine hairs on my arms contract. "Yoshi," I whisper. "Something's coming."

"Something's here." He leans out the crypt door to take a look. "Oh, crap."

Before I can ask what's wrong, he's yanked outside. As I dare to peek, the crowbar goes flying from Yoshi's hand and he gasps, his body slamming into an upright marble grave marker. That's when I register the hot, soggy breath on the back of my neck.

Biting my lower lip, I slowly turn my head and find myself confronted with a werebear. Female, I think. It sniffs me and roars in my face, spraying gooey spittle.

My inner girl is screaming at me to run. My inner Cat aches to climb.

But what about Yoshi? He's lying in a heap in front of a statue of the archangel Michael. What if he's seriously hurt? God, what if he's dead? In my hesitation, the Bear wraps a thick paw around my forearm, dragging me fully into the night.

My body takes over, and I wince as fur ripples across my breasts and stomach and my saber teeth and front claws extend.

I take a vicious swipe in the direction of the Bear's eyes, and it (he? she?) lets go, but if anything, I'm more vulnerable in mid-shift. My muscles are realigning, my bones cracking.

Maybe it's the adrenaline, but I haven't experienced a transformation this far out of control in years. I have to get the hell out of these jeans — now. I manage to leap up and backward onto the top of the Bloom family crypt, but, if anything, I've made it easier for the Bear to grab me.

"Hey, meathead," Yoshi calls weakly, crawling to grab the crowbar. "Eat this."

I'm shocked by the strength of his swing, but the Bear manages to duck in time. That's when I realize we can't let it go any more than we could Evan or shouldn't've Darby.

It, *she*, roars at me again, and, clumsily, I fight to unzip with hands morphing to paws. I can't imagine half the town didn't hear that roar.

Staggering back from the Bear's reach, I break the zipper and shove the denim past my butt as my tail uncurls from the base of my spine.

I feel the prickly sensation of more fur rising and rip off my shirt. The Bear goes down with a *woof*, and, with my rear paws, I step out of my Nikes. I want to help Yoshi, I do, but I don't know how to use this body in combat. I've never been in a physical fight in my whole life.

"Hang on," Aimee shouts, newly returned from Austin.

I bound to the edge of the crypt to watch her shoot a dart into the neck of the bucking Bear while a Lion — a gorgeous full-grown male werelion — struggles to keep his claws in the Bear's enormous shoulders.

Is that Aimee's boyfriend, Clyde? Could he really be half Possum? No one could tell that now. He's bigger, heavier than Yoshi's Cat form or mine. The mane is breathtaking. So are the muscles. Yoshi's sleeker, sexier, but I can see why he's jealous, and not just over the girl.

The Bear snaps at him, but it's no use. Whatever Aimee hit her with is potent. She sways, shakes her snout, and careens over, landing with a thud.

Swooping in fast and low, Aimee herself is decked out for the hunt in night-vision goggles. Smart call; they help her even the playing field.

"Where did you get all that equipment?" Yoshi asks, limping over.

"Paxton owed us the favor," she replies, tossing a pair of

faded black jeans in the Lion's direction. "Here, Clyde, put these on."

Yoshi opens his mouth as if to protest when he catches a glimpse of me in animal form and his jaw drops. I don't know what he's staring at. I don't know what they're talking about. Most of all, I don't know what to do.

If I retract my shift, I'll be naked in the company of boys, and if I don't, I'll be exposed in Cat form in Pine Ridge city limits — the ultimate no-no.

Clyde doesn't hesitate to begin his transformation to human form, but he's at least got something to put on. He's probably used to changing shape in front of other werepeople.

The scent rising from him is intoxicating — like mud and blood, stirred with desire. I don't blame Aimee for finding him irresistible.

I still find it odd that Clyde is a white guy who can turn into a Lion. It seems like he should be of African or Asian heritage, but now that I think about it, he's a distant cousin to Ice Age lions and, from what I remember from the Discovery Channel, lions (and, for that matter, mammoths and woolly rhinos) did roam Europe at that time.

I pace on the roof of the crypt until Aimee notices me. "Guys," she says, gesturing at the prone Bear, who's likewise looking more human by the moment. "You get the new arrival secured and see if we can reason with her. I'm going to run back to Yoshi's car and grab some sweats for

Kayla." She tosses me a grin over her shoulder. "Standard operating procedure. The pants will be too short for you, but they're better than nothing."

Thank the Maker. I'll thank *Aimee* when I'm able to talk again.

YOSHI

"THAT BEAR KNOCK ANY SENSE INTO YOU?" Clyde asks me, zipping his jeans up. He'll strut shirtless as long as he can get away with it without looking like he's making a point of leaving his shirt off.

I rub the already-forming bump where my hard head connected with the harder death stone. There's not much blood. "I'll live," I reply. "Thank you for your concern." Jerk.

Clyde didn't even know he was half Lion until this past winter. During his first shift to Simba form, Clyde filled out, bulked up, grew a couple of inches, and became a lot cockier. It's not just that his skin cleared up and his eyes went from dark and beady to (as Aimee puts it) "burnished gold." He knows himself better. That unsettled part of him, always longing to be something more, now *is* something more. Personally, I don't like it.

Anyway, Kayla took off after Aimee to my car to put something on. She's shy about her glorious, sleek Cat self and about her naked human form, which is too bad on both counts. I haven't yet had the privilege of checking out the latter, but it's safe to say I'd be a fan.

Her modesty is unusual for a wereperson, but I guess that comes from having not grown up around other Cats. At least Aimee came prepared with a few extra changes of clothes.

It's just as well. I could tell being here at the cemetery was freaking Kayla out, and that was before we began robbing her ex-boyfriend's casket.

Nakedness on top of it is probably overkill.

"Yo, Yoshi." Clyde tosses me some chains. "Heads up."

We made a lot of noise. Or at least the Bear did. The sheriff lives way over on Kayla's street, so he should've been out of earshot . . . which is helpful only so long as nobody calls to wake him up or picks up a rifle to investigate, and, come to think of it, I'm still responsible for getting the necklace off Ben's dead neck. We should get a move on.

I ask Clyde, "What are you doing here?"

"There was no Lion figure on the carousel," the Wild Card counters, "so I'm not a liability. I'm not staying in Austin while Aimee takes a getaway weekend with you."

My grin is full of sharp teeth. "Worried?"

He may be from a long line of jungle kings, but I'm the one who rules when it comes to the ladies.

Meanwhile, at our feet, the Bear's fur melts off her long, curvy body, and her paws deflate into tapered hands. "I'm worried about her," Clyde counters, and we make fast work of looping the chains around her arms and long legs, waiting to click the locks into place once she's fully human shaped.

She's a whole lot of beast woman, and we're straight teenage guys, but neither of us stare — it's not done among werepeople. There's sexy naked and there's shifter naked. I'm not saying the lines never cross (exhibit my earlier thoughts on Kayla), but now is not one of those moments.

"We packed the tranquilizer gun loaded," Clyde explains, "but not for Bear or Elk. For your problem Coyote. We didn't want to risk killing a smaller animal-form shifter with too big of a dose."

Makes sense. "On the upside," I say, as the Bear tries, feebly, to push to her knees. "There's nothing scarier than her that could show up."

Trusting that Aimee filled Clyde in on why Kayla and I were at the cemetery, I slip back into the Bloom family crypt.

"You think so?" the Wild Card replies. "There's a snake figure."

I'd already gotten the casket open when the Bear

showed up. Even with the Vicks, I will never forget this smell. I reach inside, briefly fumbling at the — God — gooey neck until my fingertips connect with a leather cord. I extend a claw to cut it, grimacing as I accidentally flick decaying flesh along with it, and slip the cat's-eye necklace free.

Partly to distract myself, I argue, "There's no such thing as cold-blooded shifters. Weresnakes are a myth cooked up by religious hate groups to —" Wait a minute. Did Granny Z say that the figures were chosen to reflect shifters who were with the carnival at the time? No, that's impossible. "There it is." Fisting my hand around the gemstone, I adjust the lid and book out of there as fast as possible.

I'm coughing as I shove the creaky door shut behind me.

"You reek," Clyde says like I don't know that. A human wouldn't catch the lingering scent, but to us, the odor is almost overwhelming. Then again, so is the scent of the Vicks. "Yeah, that's what I've always heard, too," he adds, talking about Snakes again. "But if they did exist . . . I'm not fond of anything that lives entirely in secret by choice."

Right, because even those shifters unknown to humans — like wereparaceratheriums — are still part of the pan-wereperson community.

"Let's get out of here," I say. We each take the woozy Bear by an arm and drag her toward the dirt-and-gravel road that wraps around the cemetery.

I don't even want to think about how we'd explain to the sheriff how we came to be transporting a hot naked teenage girl in chains.

She's a looker — in a warrior-princess kind of way. Tall, of course — all Bears are — with lush, curly sienna-colored hair that cascades down her broad back.

Just then, Clyde's comment about "entirely in secret by choice" fully clicks.

I say, "Aimee told you about Junior."

He's thinking about our time on Daemon Island. Poor baby. The way I see it, the Wild Card got off easy. While Aimee was forced to play the yetis' servant girl and I was being shot at and worse, he was kicked back in a hammock, flirting with a Lioness in the next cage.

I suppose it was humiliating.

Fine, it was humiliating. No shifter should be caged. But I'm not in the mood for his passive-aggressive BS. "You weren't here. You've never even met Junior. It was our call."

I'm not about to admit to him that I voiced doubts myself. "You didn't have to tell the arctic asshat what was going on," Clyde replies.

The Bear coughs, stumbling, and we pause for a moment to raise her upright.

The Wild Card adds, "Aimee is a soft touch, but why would you sign off on revealing classified information to one of those furry SOBs when —"

"We didn't purposefully reveal anything," I say, trying

to block the dull thud of pain in my head and the stink out of my nose. "Stuff was going on, and he was there for some of it. Besides, this isn't the military, and if it was, you sure as hell wouldn't outrank me. There's no compelling reason you need to have anything to do with this. As far as I'm concerned, you could've stayed home in Austin. You're just jealous because Aimee and me are so tight."

"You need me," Clyde insists. "You're acting like it's no big deal, but you've been bewitched — or something like that — which means you've been compromised. Face it, Yoshi, you could go off the rails at any moment. You've got zero distance, zero perspective. I've clocked tons more field experience with spooky magical crap, and I've got a werewolf mystic-studies expert on my speed dial."

Know-it-all. "We don't need your field experience or mystic werewolf," I reply as we reach the gravel road, where my car is parked. Kayla has already resumed human form and pulled on a sweat suit, unfortunately. I hate baggy clothes on women. I say, "The girls and I already have a plan to reverse the spell and —"

"The Wolf isn't mystic," Clyde says. "His field of expertise is. I don't think y'all really know what you're dealing with. I —"

The Bear slams her head into Clyde's and swings her chained muscular arms — hard and fast — in my direction. I jump back in time, but the Wild Card goes down. I yell, "Aimee!"

She may have learned her shooting skills on the paint-ball range, but that doesn't make her any less effective with the tranquilizer gun. It's already pointed at the Bear's back.

"Tanya," Kayla calls. "Tanya Wynne-Jones of Pasadena, Texas."

The girls found the Bear's stash of clothes and ID. They're piled on top of my car.

"Tanya, nobody's trying to hurt you," Aimee adds. "I know you must be confused, scared even. That's only natu-ral, but we can —"

"You!" Tanya points, as best she can, at Kayla. "You did this to me. You're the reason I feel this way. How dare you pretend to be my friend?"

If anyone had the faintest doubt as to whether the car-ousel brought Tanya, it's gone now. She must've caught Kayla's scent at the park picnic area and tracked the Cat girl here.

"How do you know her?" Clyde presses Tanya, pushing up from the muddy ground. "What exactly did *that* girl do to piss you off so much?"

"She . . . I . . ." Tanya blinks, hangs her head, and mumbles, "I have no idea."

The silence yawns.

"The necklace?" Kayla asks.

"Got it," I reply with a nod. I almost offer it to her for safekeeping, but the gesture seems too emotionally loaded after her reaction to Ben's crypt.

178

The Wild Card redirects his full attention at Kayla. "So you're the woman of the hour, the epicenter of this nifty pinwheel of magical fun." He grins, taking her in. "Aimee says you have potential. I'd like to know for sure. Give us the names of your favorite Catwoman actresses in descending order and showing the math — go."

Oh, for God's sake. We do not have the time for this.

Kayla steps right up to him and cocks her head. "Number one: Eartha Kitt, because she slinks across the screen and nobody purrs better. Runner-up: Julie Newmar, for posture, typically the fan favorite, but she pales — literally — against Miss Eartha. In descending order thereafter, relatively new entry Anne Hathaway, followed by Michelle Pfeiffer, Lee Meriwether, anyone nobody has ever heard of, and, though it pains me to say it, the otherwise magnificent Halle Berry. It was a mistake to totally re-conceptualize the character that way. I also feel compelled to add that when it comes to voice actresses —"

"Stop!" Clyde and Aimee exclaim at the same time.

I clear my throat. "They have a pact to always discuss animated series separately." I may not be able to follow their conversations down every odd rabbit hole of geekdom, but I've managed to pick up on most of their rules of conduct.

It gets on my nerves sometimes. Aimee is with him and not me because of crap like this. Not that Catwoman is crap. Catwoman is awesome. So is Halle Berry.

Clyde circles Kayla, nodding as if he's satisfied. "You've got huge potential, kid."

Kayla tucks in a smile, which, given his sky-high level of obnoxiousness, reminds me how lonely it's been for her, living shifter solo in an all-human small town.

While Kayla and Clyde use his phone to map the route to Granny Z's, Aimee gets Tanya into her pants and ties the sleeves of the Bear's shirt around her neck, creating a makeshift bib to cover her hearty breasts. Then Aimee and Kayla depart for the Morgan place (the longer Kayla's away from the house, the more likely that her parents will discover she snuck out), and the Wild Card rides with me to drop off Tanya with Evan and Junior at the cabin.

The Bear calms down more once she's some distance from Kayla, much like the Otter did. The farther we get, the saner she seems. And the more embarrassed by her earlier behavior.

"I don't know what got into me," Tanya says for the third time.

"Enough," Clyde declares. "You're not yourself. At least not entirely."

We take a detour to a twenty-four-hour grocery-pharmacy off the highway for provisions. All werepeople have big appetites, but among land carnivores, Bears set the gold standard. Our haul includes blueberries and strawberries, salmon (based on knowledge gleaned from nature documentaries), honey (based on knowledge gleaned from *Winnie-the-Pooh*), a whiteboard set (that Clyde insists we need), and more industrial chains (just in case).

The Wild Card snaps his fingers. "It's crayfish season."

Our five-pound order should keep Evan busy for a while.

The longer we're gone, the more my mind keeps cycling to Kayla. We still make it to the cabin within an hour, explaining to Tanya what's going on and what we intend to do about it. "That's why we need you to stay in Pine Ridge," I conclude, turning off the engine.

Clyde opens the passenger door. "Rustic," he says of the woodsy landscape and Granny Z's water-surrounded abode.

It bugs me more than it should that that's the exact same word Aimee used to describe the place. "If we unchain you," I say to Tanya, "are you —?"

"I'll behave," the Bear promises. "Sorcery, huh? Yeah, I'm starting to believe you. I caught that Cat girl's scent, and for no reason, I was furious."

"Furious?" Clyde echoes as we move to help Tanya out. "Is *that* it exactly?"

"What difference does it make?" I say, retrieving the padlock keys from my pocket.

"Let her answer the question," he replies.

"Yes," Tanya says. "No." The chains drop from around her wrists, and I catch them before they fall. Tanya rubs the skin as I bend to free her ankles. "What I feel when I look at her, even think about her, it has a touch of . . . I guess it's shock to it . . . a numbness and this deep, longing sadness. Like grief. But he's determined, too."

"He?" I echo, glancing up at her. "He who?"

"I don't know," Tanya replies, brow furled. "It's like I'm . . ."

"Haunted," Clyde concludes like he knows what he's talking about.

International News Network

Transcript: April 20

Anchor: Today we welcome back Dr. Uma Urbaniak, a university professor of prehistoric anthropology. When Dr. Urbaniak was last on the show, she told us about the remains of a 2,000-year-old humanlike male that she unearthed on a dig in Kazakhstan.

Dr. Urbaniak, I trust that you've already been consulted about the fresh remains of a white furry creature, remarkably like the fossilized one you found, that were taken by fishermen from a lifeboat off the coast of Costa Rica. Is this a hoax like the jackalope, or have we finally found Bigfoot's cousin?

Dr. Urbaniak: It's my conclusion, and that of every other expert who's examined it, that the animal is authentic and more closely related to *Homo sapiens* than *Homo shifters.*

Anchor: According to a confidential source, that's not all. It also had braided hair, its teeth showed signs of modern dental treatment, and, most disturbingly, an autopsy revealed a brain chip. Come clean: Have we stumbled upon a hidden species that's poised to take over the world and enslave humanity?

Dr. Urbaniak: I refuse to speculate on anonymous rumors.

Anchor: Then, hypothetically speaking, if what INN's source says is true, what would be your analysis of that fact pattern?

Dr. Urbaniak: *Hypothetically,* I would first consider the possibility that the new species was a rare and pampered genetic mutant or genetically engineered animal and that the neural implant was used for tracking. Like a microchip in a house cat.

Anchor: Tracking, you say. But doesn't the technology currently exist to use brain chips for mind reading and behavioral control?

Dr. Urbaniak: I wouldn't know. I'm an anthropology professor.

KAYLA

PESO IS CURLED UP, snoring at Aimee's bare feet beside me in bed. She didn't want to hole up with Tanya, Evan, and Junior at the cabin — too far from the action. She offered to crash in the tree house with the other boys, but who knows when they'll get back, and with Peter on the loose, it didn't feel right to leave her outside all alone.

Not that she's defenseless. Her tranq gun is propped within arm's reach against the nightstand. She's assured me that her friends Freddy and Nora — both fully human and therefore safe from Ben's spell — volunteered to retrieve the already-purchased carousel figures and bring them to Granny Z's cabin in a matter of hours, before the sun sets again.

Freddy, whoever he is, has the most ambitious schedule. He's already rented a truck and left for Oklahoma. He plans to road-trip all night, pick up the otter figure in Bartlesville when the store there opens. He'll grab the two bighorn sheep in OK City on his way back south, along with the wolf and ponies in Dallas, the deer in Fort Worth, the second otter figure in Waco, and the cat at Yoshi's grandmother's antiques mall. Nora's after the coyotes in Fredericksburg and San Antonio, the snake in Corpus Christi, and the bear in Houston.

I heard Yoshi say something about Father Ramos's interfaith coalition contacts — they're members of a covert group of religious types who're shifter supporters — from some of those destination cities who might be handling pickup and driving to meet them to save time. Bottom line: Not a small favor. It feels strange, being in the debt of strangers. But then again, they're doing it for Aimee, who's doing it for Yoshi.

I'm just the person (make that wereperson) at the center of this mess.

Still, Aimee seems to sincerely care about me. So far I've learned that her parents are fairly newly divorced, that she blames her dad for the split, and she prefers fake antiques to the real thing. (Her mother works part-time at Pottery Barn.)

I haven't had a friend spend the night since my first shift. I didn't ask my folks' permission, but having snuck out, it's not like I could wake them up and explain how it came to be that I invited Aimee to stay over.

On the other hand, if they find her here, it's not like she's Yoshi or Clyde. My father won't shoot her or anything.

In my platform bed, she yawns and props her chin on one hand. "Feeling better?"

I'm not sure what exactly she's referring to. I didn't admit that I almost hyperventilated in Ben's family crypt. I didn't explain that I felt awkward and embarrassed and ashamed to retract my shift in front of the boys or that Tanya's anger felt familiar somehow.

But it feels like I could. This is my safe place, and she is a safe person. I sit up, hugging my knees. "I was fine at Ben's funeral. Fine."

"I'm sure you were," she says. "Mourning doesn't always look like what we think of as grief. I know what it feels like to lose someone close, but —"

"But what?" I want to know.

"It could be that this isn't all about Ben." Her words sound bigger in the dark of my room, in the quiet of the night. "Back in Austin, protestors are marching on the capitol this weekend, groups both for and against shifter rights. On TV, Fox is advertising an autopsy documentary of a wereraccoon who was gunned down in his own front yard. Just yesterday, a dead Wolf was found swinging from a tree in suburban Seattle."

I want to protest that it's not like I'm ignorant of

187

everything that's going on. But between my parents and living in Pine Ridge, it's fair to say I've led a sheltered life.

Aimee adds, "You're a werecat, and eventually, you'll have to deal with the good and bad that comes with it. It could be that you're mourning the human you'll never be."

I hear someone settling on the roof. Yoshi's back. At least I hope it's Yoshi.

"Look," I say, "I'm getting out of Pine Ridge. I'm going to Cal Tech. I'm going to start over and meet new people who don't care that my daddy is the mayor here and who have never heard of Benjamin Bloom. Being a Cat doesn't have to change anything for me."

I don't need Aimee to point out how ridiculous that sounds.

Telling *one* person other than my parents has already changed my whole life — not to mention what it's done to the teleported shifters.

Aimee graciously tries to reassure me that I'm not completely wrong. "Werepeople and humans aren't that different. Culturally, it's like anything. It depends on how you're raised, how you want to live. If two species can have babies together, they can't be that distinct."

I gape at her. "That's possible? Human-shifter hybrids?"

News to me. It'd be news to the general population. Talk of hybrids is used by hate groups to stir up fear — "tainting the blood" and all.

Her nod is vigorous. "Kissing cousins, you might say."

She says it like she's done some kissing in her time.

"I read an article that speculated that upwards of thirty percent of people who consider themselves humans have some trace shifter DNA," Aimee adds. "A scientific article that didn't suggest it was a bad thing." She twirls a turquoise curl around her finger. "But most werepeople who claim some *Homo sapiens* ancestry tend to self-identify with their shifter species."

Might as well. Much of the general public would certainly consider anyone who's, say, half Otter a full monster.

Could I be a hybrid? If my birth mother was human, maybe she found out my biological father was a Cat and panicked at the thought of raising me. Or maybe persecution of shifters is even worse in Ethiopia than in the U.S. and she thought I'd be safer here. The thought makes me all the more grateful for Mom's and Dad's steadfast support. They'll always love me, no matter what.

Humans and shifters are basically one big family, though I guess you could say the same of all Creation. We're all children of God. I stretch my legs out and rest my head back on my pillow. "Do you think you'll have kids with Clyde someday?"

Aimee swats my arm. "You mean, in twenty years?" She pauses, apparently thinking it over. "Well, I never imagined that my future children could have prehensile tails or manes, but you know, it's not like that's the worst thing that could ever happen."

My lip quirks. Then a mournful howl rises in the distance and I stiffen. "Did you hear that?" I whisper.

"Hear what?" Aimee asks with a frown, aware her ears are nothing compared to mine.

Another howl, followed by high-pitched yipping. "Peter, I think. Howling. Will Yoshi go after him?"

A rap at the window makes us both start, and I scramble up to raise it for Yoshi. "I'm sure that's the Coyote," he says. "But I can't tell what direction it's coming from. I think he's circling the house, trying to lure us out."

"Stay put," Aimee replies. "Let him come to us."

"You think?" I say, ready to accompany Yoshi on the hunt.

His nod is punctual. "Aimee's right. We Cats rank among nature's best, most graceful climbers. We give up the high ground only if we feel we've got no choice. Peter probably knows that. He's either just messing with us or trying to tempt us to surrender our advantage. Trying to turn us from the hunters to the hunted. No way are we falling for that."

Aimee briefly lays her palm against his cheek, and something passes between them. It speaks to a shared history of pain, maybe even fear. I decide to leave it alone.

"There's still plenty of time to find Peter on our own terms," Aimee says.

We all know that's a lie. We have only a matter of hours. If we're going to replicate the conditions of Ben's death as closely as possible, our deadline is midnight tonight.

But Yoshi offers a jaunty salute. I lower the window again and settle back beside Aimee in bed. We lie quiet so long that I'd swear she's asleep, except that her breathing hasn't changed.

The howling goes on and on. It's a haunting, mournful noise that makes my chest ache, accompanied by the *click, click, click* of the bronze pull chain on my lazy ceiling fan.

Partly to distract myself, I whisper, "Yoshi still likes you."

"I know," she replies. "He likes you, too."

"He has good taste," we say at the same time, and though it's not that funny, we both start giggling, shushing each other so my parents don't hear.

I wave good-bye to Mom and Dad on the church steps after morning services and mumble something about taking Peso for a walk.

Moments later, when I climb into my tree house, I discover that a half dozen ancient-looking, leather-bound books have been spread open across the wooden floor. At my arrival, the boys and Aimee freeze in place and exchange looks. They know something I don't.

Clyde holds up a finger. "I have a theory," he begins. "I don't think the carousel figures and the ensorcelled shifters are the sum total of what's happening here. There's an attitude to the whole thing. A sentience. I think Ben is still . . ." He looks warily around the tree house. "With us."

"Ben is dead," I say straight out.

"I'm not talking about his body," Clyde clarifies. "I'm talking about his spirit."

"His ghost," Aimee clarifies. "The question is why."

They definitely discussed it before I got here. The tree house seems so much smaller than usual, filled with these strangers and their stuff and their messed-up ideas.

"Ben's not in heaven?" I breathe.

"Or anywhere else in particular," Clyde mumbles.

That pisses me off. "Ben may not have been perfect, but he was a good person. He genuinely believed that I was suffering from a curse, that he could save me from being a Cat and that I desperately needed saving. What he did, he did out of love." Not that I felt that way about it myself, but Clyde didn't know Ben. He has no right to talk. He has no right to —

"Your boyfriend tried to rip you in half using magic," Clyde practically snarls in reply. "A spell he got off of some hate site, and you're defending him on the grounds that it's okay because he was a bigot!"

"He thought he was doing God's work," I say.

"I guess that bolt of lightning set him straight," Clyde counters.

"You arrogant son of a —"

192

"Take it easy," Yoshi scolds us both. "It won't help to —"

"Hush. Just give me a minute, okay?" I say. Yoshi's wearing Ben's cat's-eye gemstone necklace, which feels wrong. It wasn't him I meant it for. Then again, Yoshi never would've rejected what the stone symbolized about me, whereas, given his attitude toward shifters, Ben wouldn't have wanted to be buried in the damn thing anyway. "This stuff is for real?" I ask. *"Ghosts?"*

"Yes," Clyde and Aimee answer. She adds, "It would help if we could ask Ben what his intentions are. By any chance, did Granny Z leave a forwarding address?"

I cross my arms over my chest. "Is that even the same kind of psychic? Aren't some of them into seeing the future and others into communicating with the dead?"

"I think most fortune-tellers are multitaskers," Yoshi puts in.

I think about it. "Granny Z said Junior had 'a touch of the sight.'"

Yoshi and Aimee both look at Clyde, who admits, "He's probably the best we're going to get on short notice." Clyde runs a hand through his thick hair. "Besides, we've got nothing else to do until all the carousel figures get here."

"There's still one unaccounted for," Aimee reminds us. "The second cat."

"Wait," Yoshi says. "What if we summon Ben and he lashes out at Kayla somehow?"

"What if, when we reverse the spell, he tries to hurt her then?" Aimee asks.

"I brought salt," Clyde says, reaching to pull a cloth bag out of his back pocket.

"There's garlic and holy water in the trunk of your car, Yoshi," Aimee adds. Turning to me, she asks, "Do you have a cross, Kayla?"

I'm reminded of the black crosses tattooed around her neck. I notice the matching ones on Clyde's neck, too. I wonder if she mentioned *The Book of Lions* to him. Given that he's being raised by Possums, I wonder if Clyde's ever heard of it.

"On a necklace," I say. My parents gave it to me for my twelfth birthday.

"Can you put that on?" she nudges. "Just in case."

I nod. "I guess."

Who *are* these people?

KAYLA

"WHY ARE WE WASTING TIME HERE?" Clyde asks, sampling his chicken-fried cactus.

"I was hungry," Yoshi says. He gnaws on his barbecued wings. "Weren't you?"

Shifters. Hunger. Rhetorical question.

"Besides," Aimee says, "Junior told me he needed time to practice the séance. He's been busy teaching Evan and Tanya relaxation techniques."

"Relaxation techniques?" Clyde echoes.

Aimee takes a sip of her sweet tea. "Deep breathing; yoga."

That's confidence-building. "The yoga yeti," Yoshi replies. "He's just a kid."

"We're here because," I explain for the fourth time from across the picnic table, "I *have* to put in an appearance" — I gesture as if to the entire Founders' Day scene — "or my parents will get suspicious. People will wonder where I am. They're already wondering who y'all are."

If it didn't look like we were out on a double date, I'm sure somebody would've already hit on Yoshi and probably Clyde and Aimee, too. Her beauty isn't as showy as theirs, but it's true and adorable and you can tell she likes herself in a healthy way.

"People need to get a life," Clyde announces. "Though that's probably hard to do in a place like this."

"Not a fan of small towns?" my father asks, strolling over. "That's too bad." Sticking out his hand, he says, "Welcome to Pine Ridge. I'm Mayor Morgan."

"Kayla's father," Aimee says as they shake. Grinning up at my father, she adds, "Clyde is my cousin."

We forgot to tell Clyde that we'd told Dad that Yoshi and Aimee were dating. Once you start lying, it's scary how quick the fibs start piling up. Ashamed to make eye contact with my dad, I give my full concentration to dipping chunks of my pretzel in mustard.

Yoshi makes a show of massaging Aimee's hands. "You'll have to forgive Clyde," he says with a wink. "You know how it is; there's one in every family."

"Shut up!" Clyde exclaims. "And stop touching her."

Dad pats Clyde's shoulder. "You tell him. I'm glad these

pretty girls have such a dutiful chaperone. I feel strongly about my daughter's personal space, too."

I'm mortified, but then I catch a glimpse of Aimee. She's looking at Dad in a longing way, like, however old-fashioned, she wishes her own father cared enough to fuss.

Granny Z's cabin windows have been covered with beach towels. Junior has a different tablecloth in each hand. He holds up the baby-blue one. "Light-colored cloth attracts friendly spirits." He pauses. "Is Ben friendly?"

Clyde visibly bristles, and I resist the urge to snarl.

"Is that a sensitive question?" Junior adds. I can tell from his posture and the leading way he says it that he's mimicking Granny Z.

Nobody answers, and Clyde steps outside.

Based on Tanya's and Evan's previous respective behaviors, there was a big debate about whether they should be excused from the séance. But we're all in this together.

Peter and Darby, too, of course, though they're elsewhere at the moment. I can't help worrying about how they're coping with the effects of Ben's spell, how its ripple effects might be affecting the people who care about them.

Meanwhile, Tanya may be taking deep, relaxing breaths, but she's still glaring at me like she wants to rip me limb from limb, and Evan's still looking at me like he wants to —

Come to think of it, I'd rather not spend quality time pondering his fantasies right now. I have enough to worry about, especially if Junior is truly capable of summoning Ben's spirit.

At least we're making tangible progress on reversing his spell. The missing carousel figures are starting to arrive. Across the cabin, Yoshi hauls the bear figure transported by Nora to the bedroom.

It joins the figures Yoshi's already brought in from Stubblefield's Secrets. It took nine trips, along back roads, in his Mercury Cougar, but we couldn't avoid the highway bridge. Even using tarps for cover, Deputy Hoover and way too many locals caught a glimpse of him driving them out of Pine Ridge, especially given how much he's been seen around town this weekend with me.

Still, there's nothing I can do about that now, so I focus on the newcomer. Nora is a stylish older lady who's the head chef at the restaurant where Aimee and Clyde work. Unlike the others, I'm not comfortable calling a grown-up by her first name, but she hugs the Austinites and new arrivals alike without so much as blinking at the weirdness that is Junior.

"You must be Kayla," she says, wrapping a warm arm around my shoulders. "Hon, I'm so sorry you've had to go through all this."

I couldn't begin to count the number of people who said something like that to me since Ben died, but with Nora it's different. I can tell she understands — not only how it feels to be caught up in something supernatural but also what loss means on a more personal level.

"Do you want me to stay?" she asks as Junior compromises by draping both cloths over the round table. "I don't know much about ghosts, but I'm pretty comfortable around dead people."

Returning with the snake figure, Clyde shakes his head. "I'd feel better if you cleared out so there's someone we can call if Kayla's ex-boyfriend goes all Amityville on our asses."

"Try not to worry." Aimee hugs Nora. "Remember, heaven is always on our side."

They're awfully religious for what my dad would consider Austin hippies.

Anyway, it seems to reassure the chef. She leaves after Yoshi and Tanya unload the coyote figures, a battery-powered radio, sleeping bags, and coolers of what turns out to be gourmet Texas-Italian fusion cuisine and bottled waters.

Junior announces that we should grab a snack if we're hungry (we all pass), take a bathroom break if we need one (there's no plumbing in the cabin, and right now, I'd rather hold it than squat behind a tree), and turn off our cell phones. He sounds matter-of-fact, like a flight attendant reciting emergency information for the millionth time.

Everyone with a working handheld reaches for it to comply.

"Does the phone have to be off to summon the spirit or just quiet?" Clyde asks.

Junior cocks his head. "Just quiet."

Clyde and Aimee exchange a look, and I'm sure they've set theirs to vibrate.

I take a deep breath. Dear Lord, are we really going to summon a ghost?

Ben's ghost?

"Please, everyone, take a seat," Junior says, retrieving a cardboard box from a nearby shelf. "Kayla, what's Ben's favorite color?"

"Dark green," I say. PRHS team colors are white and Pine Ridge green.

I peer into Junior's box of votive candles and pick out the one the closest in hue.

Then I choose the chair between Yoshi and Aimee.

As Junior pours Clyde's salt around us and the table, then lights the candle, I note that, seated clockwise from his empty chair, it's Evan, Yoshi, me, Aimee, Clyde, and Tanya. The extra chair has been set against the cabin wall.

Junior also ignites four white candles at chalk-marked points for north, south, east, and west. "Spirits are often attracted to light," he says. "And these are protective circles."

"How can spirits be attracted and warded off by light?" Tanya asks with a raised brow.

"As a nonbeliever, your negative energy is counterproductive," Junior informs her. "Now, Kayla, do you have a photograph of Ben?"

I wish people would stop asking me that. "No, I, um, burned them all."

200

His huge blue eyes blink at me, and Aimee jumps in. "What about your phone camera?" she asks. "Or . . . does he have a Catchup page?"

"He did. Does. Did." Mrs. Bloom left it up so that people could share memories.

I didn't go online and officially change my relationship status with Ben when we broke up. That would've been too public, and I hadn't been in the mood for questions. Come to think of it, I still haven't done it. As far as the Internet is concerned, I'm still Ben's girlfriend.

Aimee offers her phone, and, taking it, I quickly surf to his page, then to his photos . . . his hundreds of shots of me, with me, with his teammates, at dances, over pizza and tacos, with his tongue sticking out on the Superman roller coaster at Six Flags.

God, we had fun that day. I haven't been letting myself think about the good times.

After a moment, Aimee gently pries the phone from my hand and chooses a head shot where he's smiling. Then she hands it to Junior, who sets it on the table, screen up.

Without being asked, Yoshi unties the cat's-eye gemstone necklace and gives that to Junior, too.

"Benjamin Bloom," Junior intones, "we respectfully ask that you join us."

Tanya smirks, and Junior glares at her so intensely that she squirms in her seat. She's the only werebear I've ever known, but I get the feeling they don't squirm often.

It makes me wonder about Junior, what he's capable of. When we first met, he seemed innocent. I didn't expect him to have this kind of depth or intensity. Or maybe he's simply a great actor, which begs the question of which Junior is the real one.

"Join hands," Junior says, moving the screen to the middle of the circle so we all can see it. "Think about Ben, about how much you want to talk to him."

A cool, light wind blows through from nowhere, then . . . nothing.

Junior tries again. "Benjamin Bloom, is that you?"

Still nothing. Junior nods to me, urging me to speak, but I have no idea what to say. "Um, Ben? It's me, Kayla." My cross pendant feels chilly against my skin. "If . . . if you're here, we have . . . I have a question for you."

God, what am I going to ask? I feel self-conscious with so many ears listening.

I let go of Yoshi and reach for the cat's-eye gemstone. To maintain the circle, the Cat sets his hand on my shoulder instead. This time the touch feels more comforting than sensual, to the extent that, in my nervousness, I can process it at all. "Ben . . ."

There's no wind this time, just a more dramatic drop in temperature. Say, forty degrees.

I feel Aimee shiver beside me, but she gives my hand a reassuring squeeze.

A moment later, Yoshi coughs, Tanya begins silently

opening and closing her mouth, and Evan jerks his head like he's having a seizure.

Yoshi shouts, "I . . . Don't . . . Can't . . . Kayla, Kayla, Kayla, Kayla, Kayla, Kayla, Kayla, Kay, Kay, Kay, Kay-Kay-Kay—"

At the same time, Evan begins muttering, "La, la, la, la, la—"

"Stop it!" Aimee yells as Clyde blows out the candle on the table.

It doesn't matter. The enchanted shifters are still wigging out.

"Thank you for coming, Ben," Junior bellows. "Now it is time for you to move on."

Yoshi, Tanya, and Evan fall forward in their chairs, motionless and dazed. "Don't touch them," Junior warns. "Let them come back to us in their own time."

I've stood, knocking over my chair, backing away from the table and breaking the circle of salt in the process. "Did that work?" I ask. "Did Ben move on?"

Junior's gaze flicks around the table. "Away? Yes. On? No, I don't think so."

Clyde gets up and tears the beach towels from the windows, letting the sun back in.

KAYLA

JUNIOR STORES THE CANDLES and sweeps the salt from the floor while Clyde, Aimee, and I keep busy by setting up the provisions Nora brought. Comfort food. Call it stress eating, but I can't resist the venison blood sausage. I live for sausage.

After maybe ten minutes, I'm dialing the radio to a country station when Tanya moans. I open my mouth to say I'm-not-sure-what, but Junior holds up his furry hands, like he's trying to stop traffic. "Easy," he warns. "Don't rush her."

Yoshi and Evan remain motionless, dazed. Personally, I'm not convinced that all three enchanted shifters don't need brain scans, but I go with it.

Brushing off his caution, Aimee grabs cold bottles of water and drops them in turn in front of each of our entranced companions. It works. The *thump, thump, thump* snaps them back to the moment.

Yoshi reaches for his, rips off the top with extended saber teeth, and gulps loudly. Evan manages to unscrew the cap off his before pouring it over his own head.

I follow Aimee's lead, rejoining the group at the table, but Clyde holds himself at a distance. He sets one foot on the spare chair and reties his shoelaces.

"What do you remember?" Junior prompts. "Do you have any messages to pass on?"

"He's in me," Yoshi, Tanya, and Evan say at the same time.

Creepy. I flinch as Yoshi adds, "But I couldn't —"

"He wouldn't," Evan corrects.

"No," Tanya says. "He can't."

"But it was Ben?" I ask, holding up the image on my phone. "You're sure?"

Three nods. Dear God Almighty. *Ben.* "What's wrong with him?"

"I've never seen anything like that before," Junior says. "Never heard Granny Z mention —"

"A split soul," Aimee whispers. Her gaze goes to Clyde, and you can feel how mentally in sync they are. It practically radiates off them. "You knew all along?" she says to him.

"I suspected." He walks over with the whiteboard and a thick black marker. "Split doesn't necessarily mean evil, you know." He's talking only to her. She's the one who matters. "Especially with a spirit as young —"

"I know." Aimee straightens in her chair and addresses the rest of us. "In the event that a soul — or essence, if you're dealing with something soulless — is somehow divided at death, it must be reunited for the being to move on to heaven or hell."

What is she talking about? "Ben *has* a soul!" I exclaim.

"Of course he does," she assures me. "I just . . ." Aimee glances up, distracted by her boyfriend scribbling on his board. "What are you doing?" she asks him.

Clyde has written Ben's name in the center surrounded by those of the shifters transported by the carousel spell — each marked with an emotion: *Darby/sadness, Tanya/anger, Evan/desire, Yoshi/?*

Is the part of Ben in Yoshi the reason why he's always almost touching me?

"You dumped Ben, right?" Clyde asks. "So, he's mad, sad, but he still wants you." He smiles at Yoshi with teeth that are too big, too satisfied. "What do you feel for Kayla?"

Yoshi crushes the plastic bottle and crosses the room to fetch another one. He takes his time breaking the cap seal, unscrewing it, and taking a long drink. "Protective . . . Loyal. Like I have something to prove. I'm competitive about stuff I don't normally care about. Money, grades, being right. My glorious future, or lack thereof."

Interesting. He didn't mention the attraction between us.

"Yoshi's naturally protective and loyal," Aimee insists. "They're two of his better qualities." She frowns and asks me, "How fierce is this competitive streak?"

"Nothing I can't handle," he says. "Really, I'm good with it."

I believe him. "My rivalry with Ben was a friendly one."

Clyde looks down at his marker, and I can tell he doesn't love our answers. "I'm not saying that Ben's qualities have replaced theirs, just that he's influencing them. Or at least attached to them. Tanya, are you normally a hothead?"

She's leaning back in her chair. "I have a temper when it's warranted," she replies, defensive, like it's not the first time the subject has come up.

Clyde swaggers over to Evan, who's seated with his legs crossed and his hands folded over this lap. I've seen boys position themselves that way before. I know what he's trying to hide. "Hey, Evan," Clyde begins. "Have you always been such a . . . hound dog?"

"I'm a healthy teenage guy," is the Otter's reply, angling himself as if he's trying hard not to stare at me. "A healthy *gay* teenage guy. But I'm shy about, you know, expressing my emotions."

Clyde's grin is back. "So, it's safe to say, however . . ." His gaze rakes my body, then, noticeably conscious of Aimee's close attention, he clears his throat. "However attractive Kayla might be, she's not exactly your type. You're not lusting after me, Yoshi, or Junior, are you?"

Evan narrows his eyes. "The fact that I'm gay doesn't mean I'm jonesing for anything with a" — my eyebrows shoot up — "manly physique," he finishes. "No offense."

"None taken," Yoshi puts in, a thin sheen of sweat across his brow.

Whatever just happened took a lot out of him, out of all of them. Evan's eyes are still dilated, and Tanya's bangs are damp.

"But it proves my point," Clyde says. "Ben's desire for Kayla is haunting you."

The Otter tilts his head. "That makes as much sense as anything else."

"What about Peter, my werecoyote stalker?" I say. "Ben was never that way with me."

"That you knew of," Clyde declares. "Did you really see *any* of this coming?" He scribbles *Peter/obsession* on the board.

When I don't answer, he goes on, "Building on what Aimee said, it may be necessary to reassemble the carousel not only to reverse the spell, but also to reunite Ben's spirit so he can go into the light."

"In which case," Aimee adds, as if thinking out loud,

"we'll need all the teleported shifters here to pull it off. Including Peter and Darby."

"Darby's in Fort Worth," I remind them.

Aimee stands up. "I'll call Freddy," she says. "It's possible he's still in that area, picking up carousel figures, or, if need be, I guess he can loop around. Kayla, do you have Darby's number?"

I nod. "I'll call him." I hope he's okay. It was wrong of me to let him leave, feeling the way he did. It hadn't sunk in at the time how serious and complicated this was going to get.

I can't imagine Ben ending it all because of losing me — well, not on purpose, anyway — it's not like he intentionally caused the lightning strike that killed him. But Darby seemed incredibly distraught, fragile. More so than the ensorcelled shifters I'm with now. Who knows what his mental state was before he was caught in the spell. "I'll call him right away."

"Wait a minute," Yoshi says. "Tanya's doing a bang-up job of keeping her anger in check." She favors him with a tight smile, her hands fisted at her sides. "But," he goes on, "Peter is —"

"Peter is an X factor," Aimee concludes. "We can't be sure how dangerous he might be."

YOSHI

STANDING ON KAYLA'S FRONT PORCH, I call the Stubblefields. "Sorry to bother you at home," I say to Lula. "But I talked to my grams, and one of our dealers is looking for a mate to a carousel cat that sounds like it might've come from your set. As long as I'm out here, I thought I might be able to bring it home with me."

"We did have a couple of cats," Lula raises her voice. "Eleanor, you remember who picked up the cat figure?" There's a pause. "No, not the one that went to Austin, the other one."

She covers the phone with her hand, and I can't make out their conversation.

"I'm sorry, Yoshi," Lula finally replies. "I must be having a senior moment. If it comes back to me, I'll be sure to give your grams a call."

When I cruise inside the Morgans' house, Aimee and Clyde have already joined Kayla's family in the kitchen. The table is set in Queen Anne Fair Lady china with black trim. There's a Depression glass pitcher filled with iced tea at the center and wooden serving bowls of guacamole and black beans to each side.

Both Clyde and the mayor straighten in their chairs as I stroll into the room, and, remembering that I'm supposed to be Aimee's boyfriend, I come up behind her at the bar counter, rest my hands at her waist, and give her a chaste kiss on the cheek.

It's the kind of gesture that says I might do something more interesting if there weren't parents around, and I'm partly doing it to annoy Clyde.

She whispers, "Any luck?"

The shake of my head is slight, but I know that Clyde, at the table, and Kayla, who's depositing chicken enchiladas on the plates, both catch the exchange.

"So, Yoshi," the mayor says, "Clyde tells me you're a senior at J. L. Nixon High in Austin. They've got a great wrestling tradition. What's your sport?"

I'm betting he was a wrestler in high school. It doesn't occur to him that I'm not a school athlete. Every guy in Texas plays sports. I let go of Aimee. "Swimming."

Not really. Werecats don't hate water as much as people say, but we're not fond of it. That soggy episode at the river with Kayla and Evan was zero fun for me. But I've been told enough times that I have a swimmer's build to know that it'll ring true.

Before he can ask me for specifics, I cross with Aimee to take our chairs and add, "I'm starving. The enchiladas smell delicious, Mrs. Morgan."

I sound like a lame kiss-ass, but I'm not in the mood to chitchat with parents. I was tempted to argue when Kayla insisted that she had to go home for dinner. I can't shake off the feeling that we should be *doing* something, but truth is, we're in a holding pattern.

Evan and Tanya were playing a lively game of Clue with Junior when we left. Peter's lying low. According to his latest text, Freddy is en route with Darby and the carousel figures that had been shipped to North Texas and Oklahoma. Nora already brought in the coyote pair, the snake, and the bear. We have zero leads on the missing cat. If the damn thing turns up long distance, we'll have to figure in transport time.

I don't want to think about what our chances of success might be if we don't bring together every last piece of Ben's soul. But we're doing the best we can.

"What about college?" the mayor presses. "You a UT man?"

"I'm debating between a couple of West Coast schools,"

I say, remembering the Cal Tech poster in the tree house. Total BS; it's not entirely clear I'll even graduate on time. But if I end up following Kayla across the country, I may eventually need that cover story.

I haven't talked about the intensity of the spell, but I feel compelled to stay close to her . . . and, for some reason, to prove my chops as a mathlete — whatever the hell that's about.

"Kind of late in the year not to have made a decision, isn't it?" Mayor Morgan asks.

Playing the role of the soon-to-be-left-behind girl-friend, Aimee puts in, "Some of us think Yoshi should consider someplace closer to home." Then, as if it's too painful to talk about, she begins peppering the mayor with questions about her make-believe report on small towns.

Brilliant. I'm tempted to kiss her again for reasons that have nothing to do with Clyde.

As Mrs. Morgan muses on some consortium out of Longyearbyen, Norway, that's buying up a ton of local land, much of it from folks who lost everything else in the wild-fires, Kayla serves me and the Wild Card and herself four enchiladas. It's twice what the *Homo sapiens* at the table receive, and I suppose she figures her folks will write off his and my appetites to the fact that we're growing boys. Truth is, either of us could finish off the platter.

I wonder again how dangerous Peter is to her. I'd go out hunting him, except that would leave her vulnerable.

Sure, Clyde, being half Lion, could kick any Coyote's furry butt, and Kayla's not without claws and teeth herself, but I can't trust anybody else to handle it.

We're lingering over the last of the coconut macaroon pie when Clyde's phone buzzes. "Sorry," he says. "I have to answer this." He excuses himself from the table to do so, taking the call in the foyer. I hear him mention his friend Kieren's name and something about the national news. He leans into the kitchen, motioning for Aimee to join him, and, excusing myself, I come, too. Kayla immediately begins clearing the dessert plates.

There's something about the look on Clyde's face.

The Wild Card leads us outside to the front porch. "Thanks, man," he says into the receiver. He ends the call, fiddles with the phone a second, and then holds it so Aimee and I can see. Clyde puts his arm around her, reclaiming his rightful role as her real boyfriend. But it's not a territory display for my benefit. This is all about her. "It's your dad," he announces. "About his work. Does he ever talk to you about that?"

As the INN video loads, she says, "He mentioned that his company had been bought out. I have no idea what he does these days. Something techie, I guess. Why?"

The Barbie-esque, plastic-looking anchor begins, "This morning on *AM Live* we welcome Graham Barnard live from MCC Implants in Hong Kong. Mr. Barnard, your company is touting a recent breakthrough in mind-control technology. You do realize that the very existence of such devices is frightening to —"

"Stephanie, that's exactly the kind of alarmist accusation and misconception that I'm here to set straight. Our innovative new chip is specifically designed to modify shape-shifter thought and behavior only. Each also includes a tracking capability, triggered by elevated levels of a hormone that rises when one of the monsters begins a transformation."

"Oh, God," Aimee whispers. "Not this again."

Again? Somehow I get the feeling she hasn't told daddy she's dating a Lion-Possum boy.

On-screen, Stephanie says, "You're implying that the device could be used to protect the general public, but that presumes you have some means of rounding up werepeople and —"

"I sense that you're sympathetic to the creatures," he replies.

Monsters, creatures — nice, Graham. Very nice.

He continues, "But every day in America's cities, violent crimes go unsolved and, consequently, unattributed to the beastly criminals who've committed them. And only last week, a weretiger devoured toddler Jacinda Finch in Westchester County, New York."

"Oh, for God's sake!" Clyde protests. "That's —"

Aimee and I shush him. Werepeople aren't perfect. We've got our bad and good, just like humans. But the vast majority of so-called shifter attacks are really animal attacks or mimicry of that specific type of carnage by criminally insane humans trying to pin the blame on us. I doubt Clyde knows for sure about the case being reported (though he might, through his contacts), but weretigers are rare outside Asia, eastern Russia, and North Korea. The odds of a Tiger child murderer in the U.S. are slim to none.

Regardless, who or whatever it was slaughtered a rich, pretty, blue-eyed blond girl whose parents videotaped her every hiccup, and that means it's become a media sensation.

"Public opinion is on our side," Graham adds. "In the last election cycle, the governors of thirty-two states promised to take tougher measures to protect their citizens from the exploding shifter threat. It's just that until now —"

"Experts agree that shape-shifters are at most less than one-half of one percent of the U.S. population," Stephanie interjects. "And most live in seclusion in remote, wooded areas."

Not true. Not by a long shot. But that is what most humans believe.

"Despite the media flurry surrounding each incident, their violent crime rate is statistically insignificant," she continues. "Given current economic conditions, why should states spend —?"

"Nowhere is safe!" Graham shouts, leaping from his

chair and slamming his fists on the table. "They're every-where. Cities, suburbs, small towns. Just waiting for their chance."

"Our chance to do what?" Clyde mutters. "Hunt juicy, free-range human toddlers?"

"Clyde!" Aimee exclaims, and even I know he went too far.

The Wild Card apparently realizes it, too, and shuts down his phone. "That's basically it," he says. "Except that, oh yeah, fifteen of those governors, including ours, God bless Texas, have announced that, beginning next fall, the state will engage in mandatory genetic testing of govern-ment employees and public-school students. Which means this will be my last semester at Waterloo High, but of course everyone who withdraws to homeschool will be automati-cally under suspicion." He blinks at us. "Kieren sent me a link to that story, too, if you want to see."

"I'm sorry," Aimee says, and I notice that she's trying not to cry.

"Hey," Clyde replies, gently raising her chin. "It's not your fault. I just thought you should know about your dad and—"

"You were right," she admits. "I do need to know. I have to talk to him and—"

"It can wait," I put in. "We have our paws full now."

The plan is for Junior to lead Evan and Tanya to the

park later tonight, after the Founders' Day weekend crowd has cleared.

Once Freddy and Darby arrive, they'll load up all the various figures and haul them to the park. It may take more than one trip, depending on the size of his rental truck.

I add, "If we're shooting to replicate the timing of the spell, we've got about four and a half hours to find Peter and the other Cat figure." I don't have to point out that it's raining off and on, too, and that there's electricity in the sky, like the night Ben died.

"Make it three and a half," Kayla says, walking out her front door. "I've never put together a carousel before. Are any of you mechanically inclined?"

"I personally rebuilt my car," I reply.

"Really?" Kayla's smile is infectious, and I remember her dog-eared copy of *Mechanical Engineering* in the tree house.

Realizing we're being stared at, I take a step back. "What's so funny?"

"Smitten kittens," Clyde mutters, and Aimee elbows him.

Kayla bites her lower lip. "I'll tell my parents we're going out." She retreats inside.

"Was that necessary?" I ask, annoyed that Clyde's hyperaware of the spark between me and the Cat girl. "Do you always have to be such a —"

"Do you always have to chase tail?" he counters. "I mean, sure, Kayla is a sultry —"

"You think she's sultry?" Aimee asks.

He tosses his hands in the air. "She's a Cat. It's a Cat thing."

It's not a smart answer. Right before he and Aimee got together, Clyde hooked up with that Lioness. It was hot and short-lived. I doubt Aimee has forgotten.

He makes it worse. "You're my girl. We belong to each other."

She rises on her toes to look him in the eye. It's not the sort of thing most werelions would do to a fellow werelion, unless under duress, but Aimee has picked up a lot about shifters and dominance. "'Belong' is a strong word," she informs him. "I'm my own person. When you're lucky, I share."

Clyde's about to stammer I'm-not-sure-what when Kayla bursts outside again. "Peso's gone! My window's been busted open, and Peter's scent is heavy in my bedroom."

KAYLA

WE SPLIT UP — me and Yoshi, Aimee and Clyde, searching the neighborhood for hours. The Lopezes' gazebo, Miz Kralovansky's butterfly garden, Mr. Sweeney's prize rose garden, Bed & Gravy B&B, and behind the Bighearts' shed. No Peter, no Peso. No fresh prints around my house, either. The Coyote must've strolled right down my street, right up my front walk.

I don't care if he's ensorcelled, bewitched, or moonstruck wacky. If he harms one quivering hair on my precious Chihuahua, I will slice him into wet meaty hunks.

"Any other weekend," I mutter, not for the first time, "somebody would've spotted a stranger with my dog, but everybody's downtown."

"We'll get him back," Yoshi says as we circle around the street corner.

I appreciate the solidarity. "Competitive, huh?" I nudge, intrigued by the spell's effect on him. "And that's unusual for you?"

"With girls, definitely. Even with my sister, we never had any major issues with sibling rivalry." He rocks back on his heels. "I guess you could say I'm competitive with Clyde, but . . ."

"Standard male jockeying for dominance?" I suggest.

His eyes narrow. "Standard werepredator jockeying for dominance."

I stand corrected and appreciate that Yoshi's doing his level best to keep it under control. I wonder how much energy that's costing him.

The Cat's car is parallel parked a couple of houses down from mine. Clyde and Aimee are standing alongside it, talking to a trim, elegant-looking man with bleached-blond hair and wire-frame glasses.

"Darby took off," he announces as we approach. "As we got closer to Pine Ridge, he became more and more agitated and then started crying uncontrollably when we reached the cabin. He jumped out of the truck and made a beeline for the woods."

"Great," Yoshi says. "Now, *two* of the enchanted shifters are AWOL."

"A Deer is going to be easier to catch than a Coyote,"

Clyde points out. "They're not as smart and they're prey shifters."

Yoshi starts at that. "Somebody's gotten a big head since discovering his inner Lion."

"The term 'prey shifters' is offensive," scolds Aimee. "Not to mention stereo —"

"So is being lectured on our culture by a *Homo sapiens*," I reply. I don't mean to snap at her. It's not that I don't like Aimee. She's sweet. She's helping. It's impossible not to like her. But I hate that she knows so much more than I do, and a goddamned Coyote stole my dog. We don't have time for Darby's self-indulgent theatrics or her —

"You must be Kayla," the new arrival says, defusing the moment by offering his manicured hand. "I'm Freddy." He steps neatly in front of Aimee, subtly blocking her with his own body. Like I'm going to claw her throat out.

I take his hand anyway. He's helping, too.

"Aimee told me your dog was missing," he says.

I blink back tears. "I'm fine."

He shakes his head. "No, you're exhausted. Your nerves are shot and you're being forced to adjust to a whole new and disturbing view of how the universe works. You're still grieving your spectral boyfriend, and a handful of people you've never met before — who, let's face it, are what you might call big personalities — are acting like they have all the answers and are pulling you in a dozen directions at once." His voice is soothing. "Have faith, Kayla. Things can only get better. I'm sorry that I have to go."

"What?" I exclaim, releasing him. "Why?"

Freddy draws himself up. "Our friends at the interfaith coalition have put out the word for 'suspected werepeople' — whatever that's supposed to mean — to brace themselves for surprise visits from the state police." He glances over my shoulder at the others. "And maybe some city police officers, too. Our hometown force included. Detectives Zaleski and Wertheimer have already put in their resignations from the Austin Police Department, and they're not the only cops to do so. A handful of human officers also walked out in protest, saying there's no cause and that it's a civil-rights violation."

"Which means what for you?" Yoshi wants to know. "Damage control?"

"Exactly. Nora and I are helping with outreach to expand the safe-house system. It's about fifty percent psychology — who can we trust? — and about fifty percent logistics. You kids should be safe here in the sticks. You may want to stay put in Pine Ridge until the worst blows over."

He says it like there's any guarantee it will blow over.

After Freddy takes off, Yoshi points out what we're all thinking. "If we don't find Darby and Peter and the final cat carousel figure, then we'll be missing parts of Ben's soul, which means . . . I'm not sure what."

"Ten percent," I say. Like that's helpful. "Ten percent of his soul."

"Can't we wait them out?" Aimee asks. "Peter and Darby, I mean. They're both fixated on Kayla, right? They're not going to wander far. We could—"

Thunder cracks across the sky. "We can't wait," Clyde says. "Bastrop County has been in a drought for years. The night Ben died"—he gestures to the sky—"it was rainy. The electricity in the air may have made a difference. This spate of wet weather we're having, it doesn't happen every day, and it's supposed to clear tomorrow for the foreseeable future. I get the feeling that the symptoms of the spell are getting worse."

Yoshi exclaims, "What do you mean, they're getting worse? It's not like I challenged Kayla to find Peter and Peso before me." But from his tone, he'd clearly thought about it.

"Yoshi," Aimee says. "Your saber teeth are down. Your control is fraying."

Mystified, the Cat reaches to touch them. He looks like a CGI movie monster.

Is that what I look like at the beginning of a shift? No wonder Ben reacted so strongly.

Yoshi's flabbergasted. "I didn't realize . . ." He glances at me. "Even when I was younger, from my very first shift, I've been the master of my inner Cat."

Needless to say, a werepredator losing control can be terrifying. I press Clyde, "What does all this mean? What are you saying?"

He taps his chin. "Either the reversal won't work and we'll have to settle for leaving that ten percent of Ben's soul in Darby, Peter, and the missing cat figure, or the spell will draw the magically contaminated shifters to the carousel. The same way it'll draw lightning from the sky."

In other words, we really have no idea.

"What about the cat figure?" Yoshi adds.

Clyde shrugs. "It's an inanimate object."

Ben may never be wholly souled again. I hate the sound of that. Will it mean he can't go to heaven? Lord help me; my new friends may have a better grasp on the situation than I do, but it's clear that's not saying much.

For the first time, I let myself really contemplate the fact that a part of Ben is living in Yoshi, in Evan and Tanya and Peter and Darby.

Darby — the depressed part. Darby holds Ben's broken heart. In a way, his sorrow is hardest to deal with because it's totally my fault.

I never could stand to see Ben sad. That's why after his dad died, I took it upon myself to — "I'll be back," I announce. "I have to go to the bathroom."

I don't have to go to the bathroom, but I have an idea to investigate, and I don't want Yoshi tagging along. Eye candy aside, I'm starting to feel smothered, and besides, I don't want him scaring Darby off, assuming he's where I think he is.

I stroll straight through the house and out the back door. I risk running faster than a human could, even a track and cross-country state champ.

Doesn't matter. The neighborhood's empty anyway. And it won't be long before Yoshi and the others realize I've cut out. Of the three of us shifters, I'm the fastest, the one closest in Cat form to a cheetah. But I may still need the head start.

Only moments later I nearly run into Sheriff Bigheart's squad car. I hadn't expected any traffic on the dirt roads, between the corn- and cotton fields.

"Whoa, missy," he says, rolling down the driver's-side window. "What're you doing out here by yourself in the middle of the night?"

"Running," I say. "I'm a runner. I run." Shut up, Kayla.

"Uh-huh," he replies. "Well, do us both a favor and run on home. Somebody broke into the high school tonight and took something out of the trophy case."

I hazard a guess before he says it. "What?"

His answer is a confirmation. "Benjamin Bloom's football jersey."

Peter? Or maybe there's a new shifter in town — one teleported by the missing cat figure.

"You know anything about that?" he asks. "Everybody

would understand if someone . . . close to the boy was looking for a memento. There was only minimal damage to the door. I don't know that it would be worth department resources to pursue it on a criminal level, especially if restitution is made. Even if it's anonymous." He reaches for a clear plastic bag and holds it up so I can see the werecat claw inside. "I did find this one clue."

I've known Sheriff Bigheart my whole life. I remember him teaching me and Jess how to fish for trout on a family trip to Lake Pawhuska. He's fishing now.

I try to exude "clueless teenager." I've never been good at that.

"Uh-huh," he says again. "Well, you take care, now. Don't be a stranger."

I wave, barely breathing, as the squad car continues on its way.

When I arrive at the water tower, it's raining steadily and Darby is half hanging off the platform at the top, waving a bottle of whisky and wailing Willie Nelson's "Last Thing I Needed First Thing This Morning."

Where did he get the hooch? The last thing *we* need on top of this mess is alcohol. I speed up and leap a quarter of the way up the tower, catching a slippery wet rail and climbing to his side as he switches to Dan Hicks's "How Can I Miss You When You Won't Go Away?"

Lord, whatever I have done to have this insanity rain

down on me, I am deeply sorry. "Darby! Darby!" He's not listening. "Darby! I didn't break up with Ben because I didn't love him. I broke up with him because he didn't love *all* of me, and because of that, his soul has been split into pieces. What you're feeling: it doesn't belong to you. It's not you."

The Deer swings himself to stare at me, slack-jawed, as brown fur sprouts from his nose and cheeks. "Whoa!"

He's lost his balance. Darby's shifting arms spin like propellers, and I stretch to latch on to one, pulling him against the tower. He can't hang on. No hands. Hooves. He can't wrap his arms or legs around a bar, either. Deer limbs don't bend that way.

From far away, I hear Peter howling again, and this time it infuriates me. So help me, Darby is going to die if I don't figure out something fast.

"Kayla!" It's Yoshi and Clyde, staring at us from the cornfield below.

"Help!" I shout, holding the Deer by one arm — make that leg. "Hurry!"

Yoshi is there in a flash. It takes the two of us, each gripping Darby with one hand and scaling slowly down with the other to lower him to Clyde's waiting arms. It's right then that the Deer begins thrashing, his inner animal realizing he's surrounded by werepredators.

Clyde doesn't hesitate to jab a dart of sedative into the Deer's shoulder blade. He moans, shudders, and goes down.

I glance at my watch, realizing it's a quarter after 11 P.M. "We're almost out of time."

A car door shuts, and a moment later, Aimee comes running. Out of breath, she gasps, "Thanks for ditching me."

She takes in Darby's unconscious form as Yoshi lifts the Deer over his shoulders. "Tanya called. She and Evan are already at the park. They're hiding out on the carousel itself, under the tarp. Junior has been working on reattaching the figures to the 'drop rods.'"

It makes sense that the furry kid might know a thing or two about carny ride machinery, especially his one-time guardian's former toy. "We're still missing Peter and whatever Cat stole Ben's football jersey." At their puzzled expressions, I relate what Sheriff Bigheart told me about the break-in at the high school.

"Is the school on the way to the park?" Clyde asks.

I frown. "It's Pine Ridge. Nothing is that far from anything else."

YOSHI

LEAVING DARBY SECURED in the trunk of my car, we file, one after another, through the broken front door of PRHS, ducking under the meticulously tied yellow police tape.

Kayla's first through the door, only because she beat me there, and I almost run into her when she stops short just inside.

"Do you smell what I smell?" she asks.

I open my mouth and then I know. "I should've guessed."

"Guessed what?" Clyde asks from behind. "Can you move? You're blocking the door."

I reach for Kayla's wrist, jarring her out of the momentary surprise. "No need," I announce. "We know where the last cat figure is." Turning, I say to Clyde, "Can *you* move? We have to get out of here."

"What're y'all talking about?" Aimee wants to know as her boyfriend steps aside.

"We need to head to the old neighborhood," Kayla announces. "And pay a visit to Lula and Eleanor."

The scent of potpourri was a distraction from their werecat scent at Stubblefield's Secrets. But here at Pine Ridge High, it's a tell.

Seven minutes later, Kayla is rapping on the red painted door of the sisters' two-story Victorian. When Lula answers in her robe and slippers, she yawns, takes in the four of us with one glance, and calls, "We've got company!" With a too-bright smile, she adds, "Would y'all like a piece of pie? Eleanor's chocolate cream won a blue ribbon today. That one was auctioned off to charity, of course, but there's a spare in the refrigerator."

God, what is it with small-town Texans and pie?

"We don't care that you're werecats," I announce. "We're werecats, too. But we need that carousel cat figure to reverse a spell that's been transporting shifters to the park, infecting them with slices of her" — I point to Kayla — "dead boyfriend's spirit and chipping away at our ability to maintain and morph between human and animal forms. Or on second thought . . ." I pause, gauging the fact that Lula's fingernails have turned to claws. "We need to bring you and the cat figure with us."

Lula's looking at me as if I've lost my mind.

But it's her I'm worried about. "By any chance, after touching it, did you find yourself inexplicably and instantly relocated to the carousel? By instantly, I mean as if no time had passed?"

"Well." She fluffs her hair. "I don't know how inexplicable it was. I have been known to tip a glass of wine or three in my day, and these things happen. Not often, mind you, but . . ."

I'll take that as a yes. I add, "And is there any particular reason you decided to steal Benjamin Bloom's football jersey from Pine Ridge High?"

"Oh. That." Lula's gaze centers on Kayla. "For some reason, I felt compelled to give it to a certain somebody. I know it's strange. I can't for the life of me explain why."

I can and do — quickly. Lending Kayla his jersey so she could wear it for the world to see . . . that was the kind of thing Ben would've done. Lula studies Aimee and Clyde. "Who're ya'll again?"

Remembering her manners, Kayla introduces them.

Aimee waves. "I'm not a Cat myself. I'm just Cat friendly."

"I'm not a Cat, either," Clyde puts in as if anyone cares. "Or at least not technically."

"A Lion is a kind of Cat," Kayla points out.

"That's true," he admits. "But I'm so much more. I am a Lossum."

"Sounds fascinating," Eleanor observes, appearing in spongy pink curlers beside her sister. "What is it?"

"A leaning flower," Aimee jokes.

Lula scratches the dried cold cream on her chin, mindful not to cut herself. "I have been thinking about making a substantial donation to Miss Kayla's college fund."

"Close enough," I say. "Now, where's the cat figure?"

"Sunroom," Eleanor says, elbowing her sister. "I warned you not to bring that damned thing home in the first place."

"How was I supposed to know it was cursed?" Lula counters, motioning us to come in.

"Instinct," Eleanor shoots back. "For heaven's sake, girl, we're in the trade."

Darby's still unconscious in the trunk, but if necessary, we can lash the cat figure to the hood of my car. I follow the ladies inside. "Do you have a blanket we could use to protect the finish on my ride?"

Kayla personally carries the cat figure down the long concrete staircase from downtown to the riverfront park. I'm okay with that. It's not heavy, just awkward to handle.

She's been steadily closing herself off all day, which makes sense, given that she's about to literally confront Ben's ghost — and that's our best-case scenario.

Meanwhile, Clyde has the stirring Deer draped over his shoulders, and I'm hauling down a roll of industrial chains in case we need to restrain Tanya. Aimee is wielding her tranq gun in one hand and a Taser in the other. Lula promised she'll be here on time but flat-out refused to leave the house with gunky moisturizer all over her face. Her exact words? "If I'm going to die, you can bet your last penny it'll be with my lipstick on."

My saber teeth are still extended, and I can't for the life of me retract them. My ears are pointy and cat-shaped. My finger claws slipped out on the drive over.

"You're sure Lula is going to show?" Clyde asks, not for the first time.

"Her word is gold," Kayla insists. "She may keep secrets, but she never lies outright."

"You're sure you're not projecting?" he presses.

An argument could be made that, for most shifters, our whole lives are lies, but there's a difference between what we hold out to a world that fears us and what we hold out to each other.

When I duck under the heavy tarp draped over the antique carousel, I'm not surprised to see Evan and Tanya in partial shift, standing on its base.

Junior puts a furry white finger to his lips, though I'm sure the rest of Pine Ridge is asleep by now. Anyone inclined to make it a late night was chased off by the weather. However much Texans may pray for rain, they don't seem to know how to function in it.

Wrench in hand, Junior doesn't look like he needs my help or Kayla's. He's got some kind of leather tool bag hanging diagonally across his broad chest, and he's already managed to reattach almost all of the carousel animal figures. I can almost imagine him as a younger fur ball, learning how to do that as the carnival traveled from one dusty town to the next.

Tanya and Evan are holding up flashlights for him to see by, and there's a small camping lantern hanging from one of the bighorn sheep figures.

I turn to lift up the tarp for Kayla to join us, but at the sound of Tanya's growl, I drop the plastic and chains. Tearing off my clothes, I shift from partial to full Cat in a heartbeat, putting my body between the two weregirls. I feel my animal instincts clawing at my mind, eager to take over once and for all. I can't use human words in animal form. I'm past talking.

A Cat is no match for a Bear. But if Tanya moves an inch closer to Kayla, I'll kill myself defending her. Whatever it takes.

"Help me with this," Kayla scolds, still trying to maneuver the cat figure under the tarp. She ignores the danger, fully focused on the reversal spell and pending deadline.

But I can't right now. Evan approaches us first, and I can smell the desire on him.

It's nothing to bat away one horny Otter.

The Bear is something else. She's breathing heavy, hampered by her shift, but that doesn't mean she isn't still strong, pissed off, and deadly.

"Tanya!" Clyde shouts, slicing through the tarp with Lion claws. "Remember yourself."

Two big Cats are more formidable than one, especially when — though it pains me to admit it — one of them is a Lion. Or Lossum.

Clyde dumps the Deer and moves to stand, mid-shift, by my side. He's working the full-blown mane around a mostly human face, and, I'll admit, it's intimidating. Tanya's inner Bear hesitates, its sense of self-preservation battling with its irrational anger at Kayla.

I can hear Kayla herself whispering outside with Aimee, who must've pulled her back.

"You get in the middle of that," Aimee warns, "and you'll make it worse."

Meanwhile, Tanya charges me, more vicious from the pain and awkwardness of the ongoing transformation. She's not waiting for her bones and muscles to reknit. She doesn't seem to realize that her organs are still rearranging.

I glimpse Junior scrambling in the opposite direction and of the tarp being pulled away. I leap clear of Tanya, landing behind her, and decide to let the King of the Werebeasts get his furry ass clocked.

While they brawl, a noisy blur of fur and claws, I center myself to pounce on Tanya's back. I pause. This isn't her fault. I don't want to hurt her, but I can't let her kill Clyde.

Can I?

Nah. It'd break Aimee's heart. I make my move, grab hold with my toe claws, and cover Tanya's eyes with my hands. Clyde keeps her front paws busy — at least until she knocks him into the snake figure, which, in turn, breaks out of alignment.

My head turns at a *snick* noise to see Aimee standing with the tranq gun pointed at Tanya as the remainder of the tarp folds onto itself on the damp ground.

Tanya wavers. She goes down slowly, onto one knee, then the other.

I release her, circling behind the pony figures positioned in front of the wagon.

"I wish y'all would behave so I wouldn't have to keep doing that," Aimee says.

Kayla sidesteps Darby, who's sprawled on the carousel platform. "Junior!" she calls over her shoulder. "Get a move on! There's a snake to fix and one last cat to reattach."

Kayla hesitates as Lula marches onto the ride and makes herself comfortable in the wagon. The elder Cat woman promptly draws a romance novel from the deep pocket of her long denim skirt and attaches a tiny light. "Spell, schmell, it's just like flying on an airplane. Tell me when we're on the ground!" With that, she opens the book and begins to read.

Whatever gets you through the incantation, I suppose.

"Junior!" Kayla peers out at the yeti lumbering toward

the cover of woods. "Where the hell does he think he's going?"

Evan is propped up on one elbow. "Hey, sexy lady! Want to stroke my fur?"

Kayla points at him with one clawed finger. "Shut your hole or, so help me, your future husband is going to" — she gestures vaguely at his junk — "suffer without."

From the expression on his face, the threat is enough to quell even magical desire. He twitches his long whiskers, assumes the lotus position, and begins meditating to calm himself.

Aimee raises the snake figure so it's upright, and Kayla takes over where Junior left off, affixing it in place around the circle.

Partly forcing back my facial shift, I grimace in pain. "Kayla, hang on! I'll be right there."

"I've got this!" she says. "I can put this right."

I hesitate, compelled to help her, to prove I can do it as well as she can. Better, even.

What's more, I want to be the one who reverses the spell and saves the day. To be the hero of Operation Carousel — provided I don't kill us all in the process.

But that's what Ben did. That was his mistake, putting himself in charge of her situation. That's *him* inside of me, making me feel this way. I won't do that to her.

Am I affected by what's happening? Sure, my life, maybe even whatever makes me more than an animal is on the line. So what? This is her fight to lead. She spoke the words that started it when she revealed her secret, and she'll speak the words that end it, too.

I glance at my watch. "Three minutes, thirty seconds, people!"

KAYLA

LIGHTNING SHATTERS THE CRYING SKY. I have to hurry.

No, I have to think.

We don't have Peter, but I can't worry about that now. Maybe the part of Ben's soul that's in Peter doesn't deserve to go to heaven. Maybe it's the part that hated me.

God, I hope Peso is okay.

Focus. I click through the spell ingredients.

We have multiple images of Ben, the gigantic photos of him dressed as the quarterback, the pitcher, the graduate, and as Jesus. I move to stand next to the cat figure and tie Ben's necklace so it hangs from one perched ear. It's something that was his but connects us.

I remember setting the gemstone in the center of his palm.

I remember him saying, "That's it? I was worried you were going to break up with me."

Those words sounded ridiculous, but the next morning I did just that, and look where we are now. Ben, where are you? How did we get to this awful place?

With shaking fingers, I tear a match from the Lurie's Steakhouse pack, cupping my free hand sideways to protect the flame from the wind, and light one of Junior's votive candles.

"Clyde!" hollers Yoshi, in mostly human form again. "Aimee, get clear! Now!"

Good call. We don't want to screw up and accidentally suck them into the spell.

Clyde, still rocking a full Lion hairdo, swoops up his girlfriend and leaps all the way to the teeter-totter. Then he takes off running.

I pull the folded printout of the spell from my jeans.

I'm annoyed that Junior bailed on us and wonder why. Then again, this really doesn't concern him. The fact that he pitched in doesn't make it his responsibility, and he would've needed to clear out by now anyway.

I memorized the words, but just in case reading the damn thing matters somehow, I've got it in front of me. With my Cat eyes, the candlelight is enough.

"Blessed is the whole, unto whom God gave an image like His own.

"Blessed is the uncorrupted, he who is not soiled by the Beast.

"With these words, the demon shall be cast out.

"With these words, the soul shall be cured.

"With these words, the angels shall bear witness and deliver paradise."

Nothing. Yoshi coughs. Lula yawns and fans herself with her romance novel.

The colorful bulbs of the carousel click on; its robotic organ music begins to play.

I hold up the candle, and it's extinguished in the wind. "Do you think it worked?"

"I don't know," Yoshi says. But his teeth and hands are normal again. The fur has vanished from his chiseled human-form face.

Evan joins Lula on the wagon. They clasp each other's hands.

A chilly wind blows through, and I turn my head at the sound of Peso's bark. The pup bounds across the base of the carousel and flings his wiggly body at my legs, bouncing, his tail whipping back and forth. I scoop him up, cradle him to my chest, and that's when I notice a wiry figure in the distance. Is that? Yes, auburn hair, dimpled chin, masculine nose. It's Peter, slowly advancing toward the carousel. Except it's not Peter. Not entirely.

It's Ben. I can tell by the way he walks. By his expression. By the way he's staring at me.

All this time I've been wrong. Peter-Ben didn't take Peso to hurt him. He took Peso because Ben loved him. He's the one who left daisies on his father's casket. That was love, too.

Ben's love is the part of his soul that seeped in when Peter touched the coyote figure in Fredericksburg. That's what I recognized in Peter's gaze when our eyes met on the street at the Founders' Day festival. He was watching over, not stalking me. His note wasn't meant as a threat, but a warning against all this insanity.

Ben promised to come for me when the moment was right, and that moment is now.

Yoshi's voice is hot against my ear. "Kayla . . ."

"It's okay," I say, the cool air crackling with magic. "Take Peso and wait here."

"Kayla . . ." Yoshi says again, and I can hear the pain in his voice. It's not over yet. The spell still holds some sway. It's almost killing him not to defend me, but I don't need protecting.

Not from this. This is what I needed all along.

Steps later, I wrap my arms around the neck of a boy I've never met before and kiss the soul of the boy who was the centerpiece of my life.

"Kayla." This time the voice, the disembodied voice, is Ben's.

Did lightning strike? I don't know where we are. I can still see the glowing form of the carousel and the shifters on it, but the park landscape has faded to stars, and everywhere I look, there are black-and-blue butterflies. Our lips linger, caressing, forgiving. In my mind, I hear him say, "There's no difference between the Cat and Kayla. They are one. They are the same."

A rebellious, sassy part of my brain snarls that I tried to tell him that in the first place, that all of this drama was incredibly unnecessary, except for his prejudice and fear. But then I realize he's the one who's changed, that living inside Darby, inside Evan and Tanya and Lula and Yoshi and Peter has taught him what it means to be a wereperson.

What it means to be me.

Ben finally breaks the kiss and whispers, "I want to celebrate what you are."

I barely feel it as my saber teeth and claws extend. I don't think twice about ripping away my shirt or peeling off my jeans. I'm finally fully naked in front of him in a way so much more intimate than I imagined when I fantasized about offering up my virginity.

Then again, maybe that's what I'm doing now.

I know I'll never be the same. I'll never be the girl I was.

It's denying, hiding, living in secret that's stoked this pain.

I don't know how I'll manage to live in the world. But

raising my whiskers, I refuse to hide my inner Cat from anyone any longer.

A day later, or maybe it's only a moment, I glimpse a rush of luminescent white wings.

The park returns. The river yawns in front of me. The glow is gone.

I remember Granny Z saying that the spell was a blessing for healing. I don't feel wholly healed, but I do feel better. The grief lingers inside me, but it's retracted its claws.

It's still raining. Peter is only Peter again. Yoshi is at my side, like me in full Cat form.

His fur is black. His body is muscled and sleek. He rubs his flank against mine.

It's too soon. But it's not a promise, it's a possibility.

And that feels just fine.

International News Network

Anchor: We interrupt our regularly scheduled showing of *INN Money Sense* in light of the following footage. Please be advised that it may disturb some viewers, including impressionable children.

The scene unfolding on your screen was shot at Pine Ridge, Texas, a small town about an hour southeast of Austin, with a night-vision camera by an anonymous source. Here with me is Dr. Sedler, a specialist in shape-shifter physiology from the New York Natural History Museum. Dr. Sedler, could you explain to us what we're seeing?

Dr. Sedler: That female in the center of the screen is a werecat. You can see how she's removing her clothing and starting to shift from human to—there!—you can clearly discern her body taking Cat form. What is that odd blurring of the screen?

Anchor: Our technical crew quickly added that in compliance with FCC guidelines.

Dr. Sedler: Oh, um, of course. In any case, you can see the arms turning to legs, the hands to paws. This is not unprecedented film. Humans have recorded shifters transforming before.

Anchor: In rural areas and controlled labs, but not in small-town U.S.A. According to the source of the footage, this female shifter was engaging in a satanic ritual when—

Dr. Sedler: There's a young, solid-colored male off to the side behind her, and other figures I can't make out on the . . . what is that structure?

Anchor: A carousel. This female shifter has been identified as Kayla Morgan, an honors student at Pine Ridge High and the daughter of Mayor Franklin Morgan. Is this evidence that shifters are not only integrated into human society but also asserting political and demonic power within it?

Dr. Sedler: There's the tail! She's a magnificent specimen. Wait, what're those flashing red lights?

Anchor: The police. They're taking the werepeople into custody.

YOSHI

"LIGHTS," KAYLA SAYS, pointing up the hill. "Not town lights, something else." She sounds winded, exhausted from so much shifting in such a short time.

I can make out a rotating red light and a blue one. A white, searching beam swings across the park. "Firefighters?" I guess, once again in my human form and feeling naked and exposed next to the lady Cat, who suddenly seems a lot more comfortable with the whole concept of nudity. Lightning did strike the carousel, but we're alive and we've returned to reality from . . . whatever the hell that was. A ghost dimension, I guess. Granny Z said the incantation is shifter in origin. Tonight I sure as hell hope there's a higher power on our side.

It's Evan who recognizes the threat for what it is. "Cops!" he exclaims as Peso tucks his tail. "They know what we are." Evan takes off, running low to the ground toward the river. He's fast. Otters are better in the water, but they can jam on land when they want to.

At first I'm sure he's being paranoid. It's dark, wet, and we've all been raised to be fearful of being sighted in animal form. It's the fear that lurks just beneath our shifting skins.

I hear a splash. Evan is gone. Safe. He can go anywhere from the river.

That's when I notice Peter has taken off, too. He's nowhere in sight. Then again, he managed to evade us for all of Founders' Day weekend. Wily indeed.

Then a deep male voice booms over a bullhorn. "Shapeshifters, stay where you are."

"That doesn't sound good," I whisper as a spotlight zeros in on us. "You figure they've got long-range weapons?"

"This is Texas," Lula answers, climbing out of the wagon. "They're hunting werepeople. Of course they've got long-range weapons." She puts one hand on my shoulder, one on Kayla's. "I'm going to draw their fire. I want you two to run."

Kayla's mouth drops open. "You can't! You can't risk yourself to protect us."

"What about Darby?" I ask. "And Tanya?" They're still

249

out cold. We could carry him, but she'd weigh us down to the point that fleeing would be useless.

"You listen to me, young man," Lula replies. "Better to lose two children than four — period. The fact that none of us asked for it doesn't change that this may well be war. It's time for tough decisions. There's nothing you can do for them now but pray, and even that will have to wait for another time."

The bullhorn voice threatens once more. I kneel, and Peso leaps into my arms again.

"Think of your sister," Kayla begs. "We don't even know what they want."

"Our skins" is Lula's answer. "Our heads. One way or the other, that's always what they want. They're obsessed with being the dominant species on the planet. They'll drive us to extinction if we give them the chance. Enough chitchat. Tell Eleanor that I forgave her a long time ago for stealing my first husband. He smelled like pickles and he wasn't much in the sack, anyway. Oh, and tell her I kept my pin money in the porcelain elephant in the foyer. There's more than enough to cover that Alaskan cruise she's always jabbering about."

She leaps over us, spry for a Cat woman in her seventies, and before the first shot rings out, Kayla and I pivot in the opposite direction. Without discussing it, we're of one mind that Lula's sacrifice won't be wasted. There's no time now to process the loss.

With gunfire echoing from the hilltop, we race toward whatever future we can find. We're fast, breathtakingly so, pumping long legs, stretching long muscles. I'd be even quicker in Cat form and so would she, but again, Kayla's shifts aren't as seamless or painless as mine. I won't leave her so much as a step behind, and it has nothing to do with the spell.

It's not about winning a race or losing it. We're a team.

Besides, I'm carrying the Chihuahua tucked under my arm like a football. So I stay in human form, stay as low as I can while still really moving, using the picnic tables and barbecue grills and play-scape to help hide us in the steady rain and darkness. The spotlight swings, searching. I'm grateful for the cloudy night, the low natural light.

Trying to escape the threat from the top of the hill, we nearly barrel into its second front at the entrance to the public parking lot on the far side of the recreation area.

"Hold it right there!" It's Sheriff Bigheart, surrounded by over a dozen . . . I guess they're state police . . . all pointing guns at us. No, I've never seen uniforms like that before. The patches on the sleeve feature an American flag and read: FEDERAL HUMANITY PROTECTION UNIT.

I've never heard of the Federal Humanity Protection Unit, but they look well organized and funded. Not to mention burly. Where'd the feds recruit these dudes? The NFL?

Whatever's happening tonight, it's bigger than me, my

friends, this Chihuahua, and one recently departed teen ghost.

"We're in trouble," Kayla whispers, crossing her arms over her bare breasts.

"You think?" I reply. They don't need grounds to arrest us, to kill us. As werepeople, it's not clear that we're citizens. They didn't hesitate to shoot Lula. We have no rights.

Is Lula dead? She must be. If she's only wounded, they won't offer her medical assistance, unless it's just to torture and question her later.

We left Darby and Tanya for them. Just left them there, helpless. God.

"Come this way," the sheriff says, assuring the feds that he had his squad car reinforced for werepredators.

"Sh-Sheriff Bigheart," Kayla stammers. "I can explain."

"No, you can't." He takes the dog from me and half tosses him into the rear of the vehicle. We're cuffed and, with a "Watch your heads," forced into the backseat.

"I'll meet you boys at the station," he announces a moment later, pulling out of the parking lot. We're turning onto the road when he glances over his shoulder and adds, "They left their vehicles in the library parking lot up on the ridge. That'll buy us a little time. Somebody knows about you, tipped them off. I heard the phone recording. Guttural, young male voice. You'd recognize it."

"Junior," I say through gritted teeth. "We never should've trusted him."

Kayla shoots me a betrayed look that says she agrees.

That's when it sinks in that the sheriff is on our side.

"Junior," he agrees. "Somebody, probably the same guy, also filmed and uploaded video of you shifting, Kayla, and sent it simultaneously to every major media outlet in the world. He had great tech, pricey enough to deliver first-rate footage. You just became the most famous teenager in America. We've got no more than a four-minute window to get you kids out of here."

"Out of where?" Kayla asks as he pulls the squad car over on an unlit street.

As the sheriff exits the car, I call, "Wait. About Darby and Tanya—"

"I'll do everything I can for them," is his reply. He turns away to hug a newcomer on the scene, and then the girl Kayla waved to coming out of the yoga studio (I never forget a pretty face) — was that only two days ago? — takes his place behind the wheel.

"Jess!" Kayla exclaims, touching the cross that's still hanging around her neck. "What are you doing here?"

Before Jess can answer, the front passenger door opens and Clyde and then Aimee slide in, her curling up on his lap. "Howdy, naked people," Aimee says, reaching between the seats to pet Peso. "We've got the keys to the hand-cuffs. We'll free you once we're past the Texas state line. But right now we've got to fly."

"Don't stare at Yoshi," Clyde scolds, putting a hand over her eyes. "He's nothing to look at, anyway."

Aimee makes a *pffft* noise. "Then *you* don't look at *her*."

"My parents!" Kayla exclaims. "What —"

"One problem at a time," Clyde says. "Jess, let's get out of here."

"Consider it done," she replies, flooring the gas.

"We talked to Father Ramos," Aimee reports. "He and Sheriff Bigheart will do what they can to intercede on Darby and Tanya's behalf. But the situation is more complicated now. The interfaith coalition got hacked. We're dealing with seriously tech-savvy opposition here. The established safe houses in North America, Europe, Australia, and Asia have all been compromised."

It's the goddamned greedy yetis! I just know it.

I take stock of my allies. Aimee and Jess are humans. Kayla was reared by humans, and Clyde was raised a Possum, which is almost worse. I've coasted through school, through life. The charming Tom Cat. Daemon Island tested me, but not like this.

It's time to take up my ground game — stat.

"Jess," Kayla says, "how did you —"

"Between the two of us, Dad and I figured out that you were a shifter a long time ago," she replies, grinning at us in the rearview mirror. "Just how lousy a sheriff's office do you think we run here in scenic Pine Ridge, anyway?"

Kayla laughs at that, and I can hear the relief in her voice, the hope.

Sensing the lighter mood, Peso calms down enough to yip his approval.

"Where are we going?" I ask Jess, leaning forward. "If the safe houses aren't safe —"

"Osage Nation," is the reply, and she sounds like she's looking forward to it.

"We'll never get past the bridge," Kayla insists. "We — Wait, where are you turning?"

"Relax, sweetie," Jess says. "Sooner or later, all roads lead to Indian Country." The wheels skid against wet pavement. "Hang on, Cats and Cat lovers! We're on our way!"

AUTHOR'S NOTE

Feral Curse is set in Pine Ridge, Texas, a fictional small town loosely based on Bastrop, Texas. I borrowed the river walk and park as well as its proximity to the historic downtown but otherwise took liberties in peppering it with fictional bands and businesses (like Stubblefield's Secrets, Bed & Gravy B&B, Lurie's Steakhouse, Betty's Baubles, the Brazos Boys, and Davis Family Home Cookin'), streets and residential areas.

Like Pine Ridge, the Bastrop area has suffered from severe wildfires, though I'm not drawing on any specific real-life ones in this novel.

Other fictional locales include Austin Antiques and Sanguini's: A Very Rare Restaurant as well as the New York Natural History Museum. The International News Network and Catchup are make-believe, too, though you can probably think of media/social networking outlets much like them.

Along these lines, *Feral Curse* follows my previous novel, *Feral Nights,* and both are set in the same universe as my preceding Tantalize series. Clyde makes his debut in *Tantalize* and reappears in *Blessed.* Aimee is introduced in *Blessed,* and we first meet Yoshi in *Feral Nights.*

The Bigheart family name is Osage and is used with the gracious permission of the real-life Bigheart family of Austin. The fictional human characters Jess and Sheriff Bigheart are citizens of the Osage Nation. However, the shape-shifter fantasy elements represented in this novel are not inspired by or drawn from any Native American Indian traditional stories or belief systems.

On a more personal note, I'm fortunate enough to write in the company of four domestic cats — Mercury, Bashi, Leo, and the preternaturally serene Blizzard, who inspired a character herein of the same name.

Finally, fans of film, TV, books, and pop culture may notice nods to Jay Anson, C. C. Beck, Pat Benatar, Halle Berry, Jeffrey Boam, Ray Bradbury, Juan Carlos Coto, Joe Decker, Alex Flinn, Misha Green, Geoff Gill, Oliver Grigsby, Anne Hathaway, Dan Hicks, Bob Kane, Simon Kinberg, Eartha Kitt, Susi Kralovansky, Tim Kring, David Livingstone, Chuck Lorre, George Lucas, William Moulton Marston, Irene Mecchi, Menno Meyjes, Lee Meriwether, A. A. Milne, Willie Nelson, Julie Newmar, Joan Lowery Nixon, Bill Parker, Zak Penn, Michelle Pfeiffer, Edgar Allan Poe, Beatrix Potter, Bill Prady, Jonathan Roberts, Jerry Robinson, Gene Roddenberry, Ryland Sanders, William Shakespeare, John Schulian, Joe Shuster, Jerry Siegel, H. M. Stanley, Elizabeth George Speare, Steven Spielberg, Robert G. Tapert, Carrie Underwood, Clint Wade, H. G. Wells, Joss Whedon, E. B. White, Linda Woolverton, and Tim Wynne-Jones.

ACKNOWLEDGMENTS

My thanks to Kathi Appelt, Anne Bustard, Tim Crow, Esther Hershenhorn, Sean Petrie, and Greg Leitich Smith, the early readers/advisers of a manuscript called *Carousel*. The only surviving element of this re-envisioning is the carousel itself, and even it haunts in a new way. Thank you for helping me grow into the writer who could tell the story this was meant to be.

What's more, I tip my cowgirl hat to fellow writers Emlyn Addison, Chris Barton, H. Scott Beazley, Gene Brenek, Bethany Hegedus, Jane Kurtz, and Melissa Wiley, as well as to the Bigheart family of Austin. Thanks for buying a ticket to this fantastical ride.

As ever, I likewise remain in awe of the gracious guidance of my agent, Ginger, the diligence of her assistant, Mina, and their razor-sharp comrades-at-arms at Curtis Brown.

And of course I bow gratefully to the genius of my editor, Deb, the enthusiastic support of her assistant, Carter, and the formidable teams at both Candlewick Press and Walker Books.

YOSHI

Hours before sunrise, fleeing Texas in an ungodly crowded police car, the only thing my friends can talk about is Wonder Woman. "Diana represents one-third of the DCU Trinity, and who's her archenemy?" Kayla asks. "Cheetah. Not only a werecat, but a spotted werecat."

At least she's speaking up. A spotted werecat herself, Kayla's a lot quieter when she's naked. Self-conscious, I guess. Religious. Me? I'm a dashing, cougar-like Cat myself with jet-black fur in animal form. I love my body.

"This is significant . . . why?" Jess asks from behind the wheel. Like everybody else up front, she has her clothes

AN EXCERPT FROM *Feral Pride*

on. "Shifters are people. There are terrific people, terrible people. Most fall in between. Why can't a wereperson be a villain? Because the hero is Wonder Woman?"

"Wereperson" is a sometimes preferred term for "shifter." (I don't mind either one, so long as nobody's calling me a "freak of nature" or a "monster" . . . or insulting my hair.) We're in no way supernatural, even if our bodies can perform a few tricks that are beyond our human cousins. We're no recent mutation either. We trace our evolutionary line back to at least the Ice Age.

That's not breaking news. Werecats and, for that matter, werewolves and weredeer and Raccoons and Vultures (among others) have been common knowledge among *Homo sapiens* since the mid-1800s. Some humans, like Jess and Aimee, are cool with us, but the rest . . . not so much. The not-so-much crowd, they're the majority. Or at least they're louder.

The great thing about being in a cop car is that other vehicles give us wide berth. I don't like it, Aimee sitting on Clyde's lap with the seat belt stretched across them. We're doing seventy-five miles per hour, and I've only got one best friend. She'd be safer back here. It's cramped but she's tiny, and it's not like she has to touch my naked bod — not that I'd blame Clyde for objecting. (I am irresistible.) She could sit on the other side of Kayla. That would press the Cat girl tight against me. Nudity before and after shifts isn't a big deal among werepeople. But this is *Kayla*. I should be

AN EXCERPT FROM *Feral Pride*

getting more credit for not staring at her rack. Like a ticker-tape parade.

"Clyde, what did I tell you?" Jess moves to the far right lane to let a camper trailer pass.

"Don't touch the center console," he replies with a sigh. He's such a baby. He keeps playing with the radio, camera, and light-bar controls. Which, granted, are pretty cool.

We debated taking back roads (or at least avoiding tolls), but ultimately decided that I-35 North, the fastest route to Oklahoma, was worth the risks. Not for the first time, I strain against the cuffs and feel the metal give a bit. If I had the strength of a werebear, I'd be free by now.

Kayla and I discussed trying to shift ourselves free, but trapped in this position, my head bent from the low ceiling, our arms restrained behind our backs — no way. That's not superficial, stage-one stuff — like fur, eyes, claws, teeth. We could throw a joint out of socket or puncture a lung with a rib bone. We've got it made over humans when it comes to healing (when our forms shift, we largely reboot ourselves), but bone and organ injuries are tougher to repair than flesh.

AN EXCERPT FROM *Feral Pride*